# BACKSTAGE PASS

Dedicated to my husband, Jeff, who loves the Chosen Girls (almost) as much as I do! Thanks for all you've done to help bring Trin, Harmony and Mello to life.

And thanks to Bruce Nuffer for trusting me with this awesome opportunity.

*Backstage Pass*
Copyright © 2007 by G Studios, LLC

Requests for information should be addressed to:
Zonderkidz, *Grand Rapids, Michigan* 49530

**Library of Congress Cataloging-in-Publication Data**

Crouch, Cheryl.
    Backstage pass / by Cheryl Crouch.
        p. cm. -- (The Chosen Girls ; bk. 1)
    Summary: When a new girl in town pushes best friends Mello and Harmony
    into forming a band with her, the neighborhood computer expert transforms
    them into music video superheroes, who triumph over the jealousy and other
    problems that threatened to tear them apart.
    ISBN-13: 978-0-310-71267-1 (softcover : alk. paper)
    ISBN-10: 0-310-71267-X (softcover : alk. paper)
    [1. Bands (Music)--Fiction. 2. Music videos--Fiction. 3. Best friends--Fiction.
    4. Friendship--Fiction. 5. Christian life--Fiction.]
    I. Title.
    PZ7.C8838Bac 2007
    [Fic]--dc22

                    2006020359

*Editor: Bruce Nuffer*
*Cover and interior design: Sarah Molegraaf*
*Interior composition: Christine Orejuela-Winkelman*

*Printed in the United States of America*

08 09 10 11 12 • 7 6 5 4

# BACKSTAGE PASS

## By Cheryl Crouch

ZONDERVAN.com/
AUTHORTRACKER
follow your favorite authors

harmony

we rock!

the god of all grace, who ~~called~~ called you to his eternal glory in christ, after you have suffered a little while, will himself restore you and make you strong, firm and steadfast. —1 peter 5:10

ADMIT ONE

The Chosen Girls
7:30 pm
. . . . . . . . . .
Theater: 3-A

best movie ever!

friends
4
ever

out there it's dark (so dark)
who ~~out~~ turned out the lights?
i ~~am~~ run to you (to you)
you'll make it come out right.
   i put on truth
      and righteousness
   when trouble makes me squirm.
   i put on peace
      and faith.
now look — i'm standin' firm.

☑ clean room

☑ fix up shed

☑ go to library

☑ pray!!!

   i hope i make yearbook staff this fall. i'd love to
design the pages and choose pictures and write
copy. not the typical sit-and-take-notes-for-an-
   hour kind of class. and i'd have a real book
that i helped make to last forever!

melody

finally, be strong in the lord and in his mighty power. put on the full armor of god so that you can take your stand against the devil's schemes.
   —ephesians 6:10-11

i hope we get to go to the beach this weekend. i want to just sit and watch the waves and listen to them crashing and smell the salty, fishy water. it's so peaceful...well, it is when i can find a spot with less than one hundred people crammed in an area the size of a car.

we rock!

best friends!

# MUSIC VIDEO
# CONTEST
## Sponsored by Channel 34
## Winning Video
## to be Featured on TV!
### To Enter, contact:
## Jim Wesley
### Promotion Manager

our first concert! we are going to rock the school! i just can't wait!

# Gimme' The Beat
## Music Production Incorporated

**David P. Treble**
Executive Producer

i'm in a war (a war)
a war i've got gotta win
oh, no what's that?
(what's that?)
forgot armor again.

love the book i'm reading right now. but i feel sorry for the main character. everyone's turning on her. she's strong, though. and ~~too~~ smart. and good at everything. so of course she'll be fine. (i wish i could be more like her.)

friends

i think harmony's lucky to have her big crazy family. there's always something going on at her house. but i gues after a while i would need some quiet. maybe that's why she's always over here.

love

i want a java joint frozen caramel cappuccino <u>right now</u>! i wish lottie delivered. i'd call her up and tell her to bring me one..... please!

dance*

i <u>sooooo</u> do not want to go to the benefit dinner tonight. there won't be a single fun person to talk to. i think i'll wear my new skirt with the tiny flower print. *•* wonder if any cute boys will come.

rockin

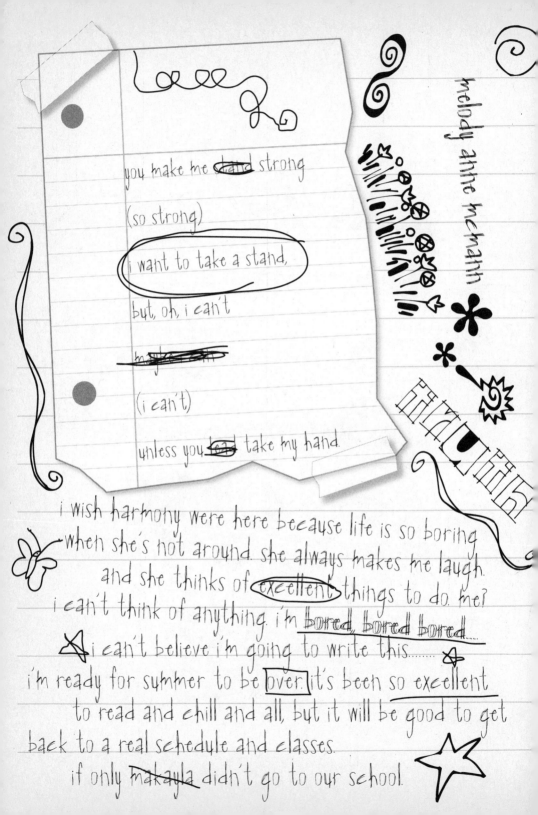

you make me ~~want~~ strong

(so strong)

i want to take a stand,

but, oh, i can't

~~m~~

(i can't)

unless you ~~just~~ take my hand.

melody anne mcmahn

i wish harmony were here because life is so boring
when she's not around. she always makes me laugh.
and she thinks of excellent things to do. me?
i can't think of anything. i'm bored, bored bored.
i can't believe i'm going to write this........
i'm ready for summer to be over. it's been so excellent
to read and chill and all, but it will be good to get
back to a real schedule and classes.
if only makayla didn't go to our school.

you know i'm weak (so weak)
i ~~ain't~~ need your mighty pow'r
can't live last a day (a day)
a minute ~~and~~ or an hour.

i ~~see~~ put on truth
and ~~faith~~ righteousness
when trouble makes me squirm
i put on peace ~~love~~
and faith
now look —
i'm standin' firm.

☑ call harmony
☑ finish blue purse
(add strap)
☑ return library book
☑ band practice in shed

when trouble
makes me squirk
i'm standin
firm

# chapter • 1

...

*My school had those flaky elections at the end of last year. You know, Most Beautiful This, Cutest That? Makes me sick.*

*Not just because I didn't get on the ballot, either. I can deal. But school is competitive enough without making it official.*

*I do know one election I could win. If the ballot said Least Likely to Become a Rock-Star Superhero, you'd see my name, Melody McMann, checked on everyone's list. Definitely.*

*I'm not lame or anything. I'm just quiet and reserved. On a good day, I like to think of myself as chic. On a bad day, boring seems to fit better.*

*That's why it's even more bizarre that it happened. The whole rock-star – superhero thing.*

*I know. A month ago I wouldn't have believed it, either.*

...

I stood balanced on tiptoe on the arm of the old couch in the shed. I could barely reach the ceiling. I had to stretch to hold the nail and hammer above my head.

Tap. Tap. Tap.

The nail didn't even scratch the ceiling. The fabric I wanted to nail up felt heavy, and my hands were numb. My arms ached from doing more physical work in the last couple weeks than I usually did in a year.

I grunted in frustration.

"I could do that," my neighbor Lamont said for the third time. He sat at the drums, banging away. His dark, skinny arms were a blur. His super-short black curly hair shone with sweat from his efforts.

Lamont's an okay guy, but he's kind of a dork. I'd never have let him in the shed if I hadn't been desperate for company.

And seeing him at the drums — it always made me remember a different boy. One who could actually play.

Lamont stopped banging and said, "You might as well let me. You're messing up my rhythm, anyway."

"As if you have any rhythm to mess up!" I mumbled.

Lamont pretended to be hurt. "I've taken two years of lessons, woman!"

It always cracks me up when he calls me "woman."

I turned to climb down. "Yeah, I remember when you started. Maybe it's time to move on. You might try —" I began, and then, boom! I fell off the couch and splatted face-first on the floor. My head missed the still-open can of buttercream semigloss paint by less than three inches.

"That's it. Give me the stuff you're hanging up," Lamont said. I felt him take the material, hammer, and nails from my clenched hands. He stepped over my still-splatted body.

BANG! BANG! BANG!

"First nail's in. You want this stuff across the whole back of the room, right?" he asked. I heard him work his way across the shed.

"Really, Lamont, don't panic," I said into the carpet. "I know it looks like a serious injury, but I'll be OK." I lifted my head and peeked up at him through my hair.

"That's a relief, Mello." He didn't even glance at me. "What's with the extreme garage makeover? You've about killed yourself painting this place."

I sighed and pushed up onto my elbows. "It's a surprise for Harmony. I'm trying to give the shed some style. Isn't it nifty? I'm going to hang up those prints too. I can't wait to see her face when she walks in!"

"When's she back?"

"Today! But I don't know what time. She's been gone forever! This is the longest we've been apart since second grade."

"Two weeks, right?"

"Two and a half. Almost three."

"Whatever. All I know is when Harmony gets back, then for sure Lamont's kicked out of the shed."

He had that right. Definitely.

BANG! BANG! BANG!

"I'm done."

"Thanks, Lamont," I said. "For a computer geek, you're pretty handy with the hammer. Maybe we'll even let you hang sometimes. We do have a whole month to kill before school starts."

A month! No more camps or vacations. Just me and Harmony, chilling out. Together.

I looked at the ocean-blue cloth. It hung like a curtain across the room, covering up my parents' tools and junk. The matching pillows looked great on the tan couch.

The shed had always been a decent hangout, but now it looked like something in a magazine. I could hardly tell I was in the garage. It could pass for an apartment or a living room.

"Think she'll like it?"

Lamont smiled. "Yeah. But she'd probably rather have purple checks and stripes."

That's true. Harmony and I don't have much in common when it comes to style. We don't have much in common, period. That's what makes our friendship so much fun.

My cell phone rang with the tune of "La Bamba." I pulled it out of my pocket.

"Harmony!" I sang into the phone.

"Hello, Mello!" she shouted.

"Where are you?" I asked. I held the phone a few inches from my ear, like I always do when I talk to Harmony. Otherwise, I get a headache.

"I'm home!"

"Excellent!"

"Sí! Can I come over?"

"Definitely! I'm dying to see you."

"Cool frijoles. It's been hundreds of years! Meet me halfway?"

I looked at the stack of art prints. "Uh … I'm kinda working on something. Do you mind just meeting me at the shed?"

"Give me fifteen minutes," she said and hung up.

I scrambled up and grabbed a botanical print off the coffee table. Very elegant.

"She's home, Lamont! Harmony's back! She's coming in fifteen minutes! Hurry! Help me get this artwork hung."

He started nailing. "You recovered pretty fast," he commented.

"Just be quiet and help me. I want this place perfect when she gets here."

Turns out, I didn't need to rush. After helping me hang pictures, hide paint cans, and touch up the trim, Lamont left. As he headed out he said, "I'm outie. Tell Harmony 'hey' for me. You two will wanna do that girl talk stuff, anyway." For a guy, Lamont has a decent amount of brains.

Half an hour after he left, I was still wandering around fluffing pillows and rearranging magazines. I figured Harmony had gotten stuck doing the family thing. She has a huge family.

I went crazy waiting. We live only three blocks apart. Of course, the blocks are long blocks. What could possibly happen to someone walking alone . . .

*What could happen?* I thought. Oh, no. All kinds of terrible things could happen. What was I thinking? Why hadn't I called?

I whipped out my cell phone and clicked on her cross-eyed picture. Her phone rang three times. I tried to prepare myself for the worst. Maybe a scary voice saying, "I have Harmony. Put five thousand dollars in small bills inside a black briefcase —"

"Hello, Mello!"

"Harmony?"

"Yeah. Oh, no! I should have called. I'm so sorry. I've been, um . . . listen. I'm coming now, OK, and I'm going to surprise you."

I realized I'd been holding my breath and exhaled. Then I looked around the shed again and grinned. "And I'm going to surprise you too!" I said.

"Great. Be right there."

I sat down and drummed a beat on the coffee table.

Finally, I heard a knock.

I ran over (tripping only once) and flung the door open.

And I froze.

The tall girl with the mass of hot-pink hair and the perfect smile couldn't be Harmony. Definitely not.

I had never seen this girl in my life.

# chapter • 2

...

Still wednesday

"So what do you think?" the pink-haired, totally glam girl said.

I tried to decide where to begin with my questions. Who in the world are you? What are you doing at the shed in my backyard? Where is my best friend?

Before I could get a word out of my mouth, she started talking. "It's me: Harmony. I know everyone thought I went to my aunt's house. But really, I've been on one of those extreme makeover shows! I got the works: hair extensions, color, contacts, plastic surgery here and there ... so, do you like it?"

I felt my mouth hanging open. I knew I looked like an idiot, but I was confused.

My best friend left town two and a half weeks ago. When she left, she was a short Hispanic girl with chin-length black wispy hair and gray eyes. Now this tall, pale, pink-haired person claimed to be her.

I've seen makeover shows. Even they couldn't turn Harmony into the girl in front of me. This had to be a joke.

But somewhere in the back of my mind I wondered where the TV crew was hiding, recording my reaction. I could hear the voice-over in my mind: *Her friend Mello is amazed and stunned. Hey, it looks like Mello could use a makeover herself. Let's do something with that long, straight hair. And is that buttercream paint smeared on her clothes?*

I'm glad I never got any words out, because it would have made things worse. See, right then, the pink-haired girl almost died laughing. "Your face!" she said. "It's priceless!"

Then Harmony—my Harmony—came running around the corner of the building. "Hello, Mello!" she said and threw her arms around me. Then she pulled away, laughing so hard she accidentally shot snot out of her nose. She does that sometimes. It always makes her laugh even harder. Usually it happens when she and I are laughing together. But this time she and the pink girl were laughing together, and I was the one they were laughing at.

"This is Trin," Harmony said when she could breathe again. "I ran into her on my way over, and we started talking. You won't believe this! She just moved in across the street from me."

At that point Trin took over. "My real name's Trinity, but everyone calls me Trin," she said, still giggling. "We just moved here from Dallas. You know, in Texas. And I was out jogging, and ohwow, it's so beautiful here, but it's hot today! Raise your hand if you think I was dumb to be out jogging in the middle of the day."

I started to raise my hand, but she kept talking. I guess she didn't actually want us to vote.

"When I saw Harmony, she looked so nice, so I just said 'hi.' And she said 'hi' back, and we started talking. I'm sure I totally lost my aerobic heart rate. I'm so psyched you two go to the same school I'll be going to, and you're in the same grade! Is this sweet or what?" She pronounced "sweet" with two syllables, like this: *suh-weet*. How irritating.

When she finally quit talking, Trin smiled an absolutely brilliant smile at me. Then she smiled at Harmony and threw an arm around her. She looked like ... like she had been best friends with Harmony since second grade.

"Did you say you moved here?" I asked, aware of how stupid I sounded.

Another megawatt smile. "Yeah. Just last week. I love it here. California is way fabulous."

I knew I should return the smile, but I couldn't get the message to my face. I guess Harmony noticed I needed help. "When you called, I thought it would be so funny to trick you! I mean, look at her." She pulled away from Trin and looked her up and down. "Could you find anyone more opposite from me?" She and Trin exploded into spasms of laughter again.

I felt sick. I hadn't even fallen for their dumb trick, but of course it wouldn't help to say that now.

I forced myself to smile, and I even tried to laugh. The laugh felt like it might turn into a sob, though, so I quit.

"So are you going to let us in?" Harmony asked. "I told Trin all about you and how cool the shed is."

I thought of the buttercream paint and the blue cloth, and how the shed had always belonged to Harmony and me. And I looked at Harmony and tried to make her read my mind: *No. I'm not going to invite that girl in. She doesn't belong. We belong.*

It didn't work. Harmony just smiled at me.

So I said, "Yeah, come on in." Then I looked at Trin and lied a little bit. "It's nice to meet you," I said, backing up as they burst through the doorway.

"Mello!" Harmony yelled. "This is rockin'! Major decor!" She oohed and ahhed until it got embarrassing.

Trin seemed to like it too. "Sweet! This is amazing. It's like a little house. Ohwow, I'd love to have this in my backyard. You really get this whole place to yourselves?" she asked.

I wanted to say, "Up until five minutes ago."

Harmony said, "The shed is the best thing since buttered bread."

"Sliced bread, Harmony," I corrected.

Trin picked up a drum stick and tapped on a snare. "Who plays the drums?"

I shot Harmony a keep-your-mouth-shut look. "Lamont tries to play them. He's my neighbor."

"Sweet. I play electric guitar."

"No way!" Harmony screamed happily. "I play bass!"

They went crazy with guitar talk until Harmony finally plopped down on the couch and picked up a pillow. "So tell me everything, Mello! I can't believe my cell wouldn't work out there. This has been the longest two and a half weeks ever."

"Oh, I don't know. Not much has happened," I said. Another lie. But did Harmony really expect me—in front of a stranger—to go into the details of seeing Cole Baker at the mall wearing that red long-sleeved T-shirt with the navy stripe that makes him look sooo cute? I definitely didn't plan to tell about tripping over a tree (it was a very small tree!) in front of the library. Or the snotty comment Makayla made at the Java Joint.

It was worse than Harmony being gone. She sat there in the shed, and all the things I'd saved up to tell her seemed dumb instead of exciting or funny. Our reunion was ruined.

"Tell me about Tia Isabella's," I said, to throw her off. That's the best thing about talkative people. They're usually happy to talk about themselves.

So Harmony told us all about her visit to her aunt's house. Her aunt is single with no kids. Each summer one kid in Harmony's family (there are five of them) gets to go see her. She spoils them rotten for a few weeks.

Harmony is really funny. She had a great trip, and after a while I forgot about Trin and just laughed at Harmony's stories.

Until Trin said, "Harmony, are your hands blue? Maybe it's just the light in here, but they look blue to me."

Harmony held her hands in front of her face. She looked surprised. "Sí. They're blue."

I got out of my chair and walked over to Harmony. I took one of her hands in mine. It had a slightly blue tinge to it. "Why are they blue?" I asked.

"Yo que se! How should I know?"

Trin said, "Oh wow. This is not good at all. But let's not panic. Harmony, how do you feel? Do you feel dizzy or light-headed?"

Harmony scrunched her eyebrows together. "Maybe a little."

"Oh, no." Trin closed her eyes. She started twirling a piece of hair around her finger. She opened her eyes and said, "Is it hard to breathe?"

Harmony's surprised look changed to a worried look.

I could hear her short, fast breaths. "Sí. Now that you mention it."

Trin shook her head and made clucking noises with her tongue. "I was afraid of that. That's a very bad sign. Do you feel cold?"

Harmony shivered. "A little."

"The fan is pointing straight at her," I pointed out.

Neither of them seemed to hear me. Trin looked at Harmony's face. "I'm surprised your face isn't blue too. But you do look a little pale. Here, lie down." She moved a pillow to one end of the couch and pushed Harmony's head onto it. Then she grabbed another pillow and put it at the other end of the couch. She scooped up Harmony's feet in her long arms and heaved them onto the second pillow.

Then she screamed. "Aaaaaah!"

I jumped.

"Ohwow, look at her legs! They're worse than her hands!"

I looked. Trin busily rolled up Harmony's pant legs, so I could see very clearly that Harmony's legs were definitely blue.

Harmony sat up, looked at her legs, and screamed, "What is wrong with me?" Her breathing got louder and faster.

Trin looked at me. "Do you have a phone in here?" she asked.

"Yes. I've got my cell."

"Call 9-1-1."

Harmony sat up. "9-1-1?"

Trin pushed her back down. "Yes, 9-1-1."

"Why don't I just get my mom?" I asked. "Think about it. Harmony can't be that bad. She was fine a couple minutes ago."

Trin shook my shoulders and yelled into my face, "We don't have time to think! Harmony is going into respiratory arrest! It can happen fast like this. She needs immediate medical attention. Call now!"

I asked, "Respiratory arrest? How do you know?"

"I've seen this exact thing on *Real Emergencies*. It was a baby. The ambulance barely got there in time. They said if the mom had called one minute later the baby would have died. Hurry up!"

I looked at Harmony, pale and panting and blue on the couch. "What do you think, Harmony?" I asked.

She started crying. "I'm scared, Mello. My hands feel all tingly."

I didn't think Harmony was dying, but I couldn't lose her. I definitely couldn't lose her. I found my phone and dialed 9-1-1.

"This is so awful," Trin whispered. She started crying too. "I can't lose my first friend in town. Have they answered? Tell them we have a female in respiratory arrest."

I repeated the information to the operator, who asked a series of questions: "Is she choking? Is she struggling to breathe?" The whole time Trin kept yelling stuff at me. "Did you tell them she's turning blue? Tell them she's dizzy."

I could hardly hear the operator and Trin at the same time. Harmony looked worse and worse. It was definitely very stressful.

I gave the woman my address and told her we were in the garage behind the house. "The numbers on our street are weird," I remembered to explain. "They don't go in order, so pizza guys always get lost."

"Get out there and wave them in!" Trin yelled. "We don't have any time to lose!"

I headed for the street.

"Wait!" Trin called. "Take something bright so they see you. A red scarf or something."

I almost said, "Why don't you go? They can't miss your hair." But I looked at Harmony and decided this wasn't the time to start a fight.

"They'll see me. I'll make sure," I said instead. I ran out to the curb.

I heard the sirens before I saw the ambulance. My heart pounded. Time seemed to slow down.

The ambulance driver looked right at me and turned in at our driveway, lights flashing and sirens blaring. My parents came running out of the house, and I called, "It's Harmony. She's not breathing right."

The medics jumped out, and I pointed them to the garage.

Mother said, "I'll call Mrs. Gomez," and ran back into the house.

Dad came and wrapped me in a hug. Then we headed for the garage.

The medics already had Harmony on a stretcher. A short, stocky man checked her blood pressure and called out, "One forty over ninety."

A dark-haired woman said, "Respiration's one hundred twenty. The patient is hyperventilating." She got a mask and held it over Harmony's nose. "Her coloring appears normal, other than her hands and legs."

The first man checked Harmony's pulse in her wrist and her ankle. "Pulses are normal. I'll begin the IV." He cleaned her hand with some kind of cotton swab.

He looked at the swab. "This blue is coming off," he said.

Harmony tried to talk. The lady pulled the mask away.

"The blue is coming off?" Harmony asked. "How can it come off?"

"Well, sweetheart," the medic-lady answered, "are these new pants you have on?"

We all looked at the blue pants Harmony wore.

"Sí," Harmony said. "Tia Isabella got them for me."

"Did you put your hands in your pockets?" the lady asked. "I think the dye from your new pants came off on your skin."

Harmony looked at her hand where the man had rubbed a spot clean. "But if that's all that was wrong, why couldn't I breathe? Why did my hands tingle?"

The man spoke up. "I think you got scared. That made you hyperventilate."

"She did get scared," I offered. I pointed at Trin. "Trin saw the blue. She said Harmony was in respiratory arrest. She scared both of us."

*She's in trouble now*, I thought. Maybe they'll load her into the ambulance and drive her straight to jail for wasting their valuable time over something as dumb as clothing dye.

Instead they started laughing. Hard.

My dad joined in with his deep, hearty laugh.

Trin looked around the room, confused. Then she said, "Ohwow. Raise your hand if you've ever been so embarrassed!" and she laughed too.

Even Harmony laughed, there on the stretcher, until the medic helped her down.

When my mother rushed in with Mrs. Gomez, expecting to find Harmony dying, they found a roomful of people laughing instead.

I seemed to be the only one who didn't find it funny. In fact, now that I knew Harmony was okay, I had time to think about how scary it had all been. I would be so alone if I lost her.

And in the middle of all those laughing people, I started bawling my head off. I blubbered like a big baby.

Harmony said, "Oh, Mello!" and gave me a hug.

But when her mom said it was time to go, Harmony threw her arm around Trin and said, "Come on, neighbor, we'll give you a ride home. I'll be 'blue' if you don't come with me!"

They started laughing again. Trin said, "I'd just 'dye' if I had to walk!"

I looked at them walking out together and thought, *I feel like I did lose Harmony today, after all.*

# chapter • 3

• • •

The next morning I sprinkled allspice on my blueberry oat-meal and settled into the den sofa to read my new book and listen to my iPod. Then the phone rang.

"Hello, Mello!"

"Hey, Harmony."

"Do you realize we only have a month until school starts? We haven't even planned our strategy!"

"Why do we need a strategy?"

"We have to have a plan! How to avoid Makayla and the Snob Mob. How to make sure we see Cole at least twice a day. How to be the cutest, coolest girls at James Moore. We need to prepare! You know what they say: A bird in the hand is worth two in the nest."

"In the bush, you mean."

"Why the bush? Birds live in nests."

She had a point there.

I smiled. "So when are you coming over?"

"Right now, of course! Meet me halfway?"

"Definitely."

I headed up the hill on the long sidewalk. What a relief to see Harmony rounding the corner — alone.

By the time we got to the shed, I'd already told her about Cole at the mall, and tripping over the tree, and Makayla's rude comment. Harmony laughed in all the right places, the way she had since we were seven years old. Harmony Gomez and I were born to be best friends, and nothing could change that.

Harmony lugged her bass guitar case on one shoulder. "I thought we might need musical inspiration," she explained. She had a huge bag slung over her other shoulder.

"Need help?" I asked.

"Sí," she answered, handing me the bag. "But no peeking!"

When we got to the shed, she put her guitar down and reached for the bag. She pulled out a DVD: *Body of Steel.* "This aerobic workout is step one in our plan to be the cutest girls at James Moore. If we do this workout every day, we'll be able to outrun the Snob Mob during PE."

"Harmony, it's summer! The best thing about summer is there's no PE. We can be lazy bums. Besides, I'm not sure the Snob Mob care how fast we can run the mile," I pointed out.

Harmony pulled out a package of chocolate-covered pretzels. Harmony is a serious chocoholic and I love pretzels, so chocolate-covered pretzels are our official number-one snack. She waved the package in front of me. "Maybe not, Mello, but if we do the workout, we can enjoy some serious snackage without guilt. No pain, no pretzels."

She turned the TV to channel 3 and popped in the DVD. Then she took her bag and disappeared behind the newly hung blue cloth.

She came out with a bright purple terrycloth sweatband on her head and matching leg warmers on her calves. "Do I look like an aerobics queen, or what?"

"Harmony, you look like someone in an antique dancer movie, you goober."

"But I am not to be the only goober. Look!" She reached into her bag again and pulled out aqua leg warmers and a sweatband. She held them out for me.

"No way. Definitely not. I am not the sweatband kind," I said, laughing.

Harmony doesn't give up easily. She walked over and pulled the sweatband onto my head. "You are very elegant, Mello," she said. "But you have a lot to learn about fashion." She shoved my sneaker through a leg warmer, continuing, "Fashion doesn't have to be limited to expressing who you are. Fashion can express who you want to be." Then she rolled the other leg warmer over my other shoe.

"Right now, we want to be the queens of fitness. So we put this stuff on, and we become the queens of fitness." She stood back to look me over.

"Perfecto!"

"Did I say I wanted to be a queen of fitness?" I asked, pulling the things up my legs.

"Quiet! We've missed half the warm-up. Come on."

She started right in, moving just like the woman on the screen. I stood behind her, going right when I should go left and raising my arms when they were supposed to be down. I hate aerobics.

Fifteen minutes into the workout, we queens of fitness became the pooped princesses. "Forget this!" Harmony declared. "This workout was created by an evil-minded dictator." She turned off the video and grabbed the pretzels. "We've totally earned these."

"You're giving up?" I asked. "What about your inspirational headband?"

"Oh, eat a pretzel. You talk too much, Mello."

Someone knocked at the door. "It must be Lamont," I said. "He had to leave before you got here yesterday."

"You let Lamont in the shed?" she asked.

"You were gone almost three weeks, Harmony! I had to talk to someone."

The person knocked again.

Harmony looked at me. "I can't move. Can you?"

I groaned and pulled myself up off the couch. I limped over and opened the door.

There stood Trin in all her glory. She looked like she'd been up since five a.m. doing her hair.

I, on the other hand, had not even showered yet. I had on a headband and leg warmers that had gone out of style twenty-five years ago. And despite the headband, I felt sweat running down my face.

"Hey, Mello," she said, stepping inside. "You look, uh, cute. Harmony, I tried to call your cell, but you didn't answer."

"Oh! I forgot it." Harmony had managed to whip off her headband and leg warmers.

"There probably wasn't room in your bag with all the leg warmers you brought," I suggested.

Trin said, "When I couldn't get you, I went to your house. I just couldn't sit at home for another second. Ohwow, it's boring. And my little brother keeps making me play Matchbox cars. Raise your hand if that's the last thing you want to do. So anyway, your sister said you were here. I hope you guys don't mind me barging in. I brought my guitar." She said that as if it justified her presence in the shed.

"Cool frijoles!" Harmony said, suddenly energized. She jumped off the couch and started taking her bass out of the case.

I crossed my arms. "I thought you couldn't move."

Harmony looked surprised. "I couldn't when I thought it was Lamont." She showed Trin where to plug in. They messed around, tuning and testing amps. I limped back over to the couch and sat down. I pulled off the headband and started on the leg warmers.

Trin looked at me with pity in her eyes. "It's too bad you don't play an instrument."

"Actually — ," Harmony began.

I interrupted quickly. "Actually, I played violin for a year. I hated practicing, so I quit."

Trin nodded.

The two of them started a song. Harmony kept saying, "This is so cool. I've never played with a lead guitar. We can seriously jam."

Trin said, "Harmony, you're incredible! I can't believe we both play guitar."

After the first song Trin said, "It's so good to hang with someone my age. My brother is only six, and sometimes he drives me crazy!"

Harmony said, "No way! I have a six-year-old brother too. He always has a costume on. And he thinks he really is that person he's dressed up like, you know?"

"What about you, Mello?" Trin asked. "Any brothers or sisters?"

"Nope. It's just me," I answered.

"Do you know 'Day after Day'?" Harmony asked quickly. "Let's try it in G."

Since it's an easy song, they talked while they played. "Where did you get that cool shirt, Trin?"

"There's a great shop in Dallas called Totally Tees. Ohwow, our mall there was great! But I can't wait to hit the mall here," Trin answered.

Harmony smiled. "Let's go together. I love to shop!"

Trin looked at me while she strummed her guitar. "Are you a serious shopper too, Mello?"

Harmony answered for me. "Mello hates shopping. She's so picky she can never find anything she likes."

"Oh. So are you in dance or anything?"

I shook my head. "I'm not coordinated enough," I explained.

Harmony finished the song and put down her guitar. She did a pirouette. "I used to take ballet—it helped my balance for karate."

"Awesome! I love ballet, and I haven't found a studio here yet. Maybe I can take where you used to go. Ohwow, can you believe we have so much in common?"

I looked at Trin's delighted face. I always loved it that Harmony and I are so different. Maybe that's not as great as I thought.

I started playing a game on my phone. Every once in a while Harmony would say, "What do you think, Mello?" and I would say, "It sounds great." Which was true. They sounded like they had played together forever. In fact, I had to concentrate to keep my feet still. But I refused to let them see me get into their music.

I thought since Harmony had been my best friend for years she might be able to tell I was bored. Maybe she'd suggest we do something else for a while or, better yet, suggest Trin go unpack a few boxes at her new house.

Once Harmony said, "We could sure use some drums, huh?"

I just rolled my eyes. "Want me to go get Lamont?"

Harmony actually stuck her tongue out at me. How immature!

She finally complained that her fingers hurt. I hoped Trin would take the hint and go home. They both started putting their guitars away.

"Who's John?" I asked.

Trinity looked at me, her big purple eyes totally blank. "Huh?"

I guess she forgot that her black guitar case had the name "John" written across it in huge white letters. "Your case," I said, pointing.

"Oh!" She turned the case over. The other side had "15:16" written in hot pink. "It's my life verse."

She said that like everyone has a life verse. I had no idea what it was, but I didn't want to look stupid (again) so I nodded and said, "Excellent." Then I waited, nervous, to see if she'd ask me what mine was.

She didn't. She did walk over and reach for a pretzel.

I grabbed the package and zipped the top closed.

She dropped her hand and turned toward Harmony. "Do you have any peanuts? Ohwow, I just love peanuts."

"We never eat peanuts," I answered.

"Do you want to walk us halfway?" Harmony asked me.

So she wanted to leave with Trin. So much for planning our strategy to be the coolest girls at James Moore.

Or maybe Harmony's new strategy involved trading a somewhat boring friend for one who was already cool and cute. I just nodded and picked up Harmony's bag.

I listened to them talk as we walked, but about halfway, I looked right at Harmony and said, "See you tomorrow?"

She said, "Cool frijoles."

And Trin said, "That sounds sweet. Let's bring our guitars again."

I stomped all the way back to the shed. I went inside and picked up the drumsticks.

Then I sat at the drums and played until my arms hurt.

# chapter • 4

...

I spent the next morning trying to think of a reason—any reason—not to join the jam session in the shed. In desperation, I finally asked Mom if she needed help with anything around the house.

"No, sweetheart," she answered. "I'm going up to your father's office in a bit. I know, why don't you put on a dress and come with me? Today is the ribbon-cutting ceremony for that new office complex. You can stand up with us. The voters love to see your picture in the newspaper."

"Um, no, I guess I better hang around here," I mumbled. "Harmony might come by."

I knew I could think of something better than a ribbon-cutting. I love my dad, but I don't love that he's the mayor.

My phone rang with the first few bars of "La Bamba." Crud. I didn't have an excuse ready.

"Hello, Mello!"

"Hey, Harmony."

"Let's go to Java Joint. I haven't had a chocolate mocha freeze in almost a month. Can you be ready in thirty minutes?"

"That sounds excellent."

"Bueno. We'll come by for you."

She hung up before I could ask who "we" were. Like I had to ask.

At least this time I had some warning before I had to face fashion-plate Trin. I pulled on my favorite brown cropped pants with the lace trim. Then I found my brown stretch tee and the lace mini-vest.

I smiled when I looked in the mirror. I finished the last curl and pulled a clump of hair into a clip just as the doorbell rang. On my way out the door, I kissed Mom and said, "Have fun cutting ribbons!"

Trinity smiled her toothpaste-commercial smile at me. "Mello, you look great! You have such classic features. And cocoa is a great color on you."

I wondered what her deal was. Still, it did feel good to get a compliment from someone as together as Trin. Harmony always says I'm pretty, but she has to say that stuff because she's my best friend.

We walked down the hill. I pointed to Lottie's house as we passed it. "Have you prepared Trin for Lottie?"

Harmony laughed. "Mello's neighbor Lottie owns the Java Joint," she said.

Trin said, "Sweet."

"Lottie is a little different," I explained. "She could definitely benefit from a makeover."

"She's super pale, and she wears a slice of bright pink rouge on each cheek and tons of sky-blue eye shadow," Harmony added.

We stopped at the corner and waited for a car to pass. Then we started up the next hill.

"But she loves us," I said.

"And we love her frozen coffees and smoothies!" Harmony declared.

We turned right at the top of the hill and walked the last block to Java Joint.

"How's my girls?" Lottie squealed as we came in. "Oh, Harmony, me and Mello's been missing you something fierce! So glad you're finally back. Well, lands' sakes, lookie here! There's another one!" She fixed her beady brown eyes on Trin. "Who on earth is this?"

My feelings exactly.

Harmony said, "This is Trin. She just moved here from Texas."

"Well, I'll be! Ain't you a cutie? So my girls are taking you in, are they? That sounds like my girls. Good girls with good hearts. Always thinking of others." She smiled, and her eyes were swallowed up in wrinkles.

"Oh, lands. I remember moving when I was in ninth grade," Lottie continued. "Scariest time of my life. Had to leave all my friends behind — there were loads of them too. I was the most popular girl in school. Yes, I was."

Harmony and I grinned at each other. Lottie told us often about how pretty and popular she had been as a girl. It didn't seem possible that the lady in front of us had ever been either.

"You don't believe me now, do you? You think Lottie's makin' this stuff up." Lottie rolled her eyes, and the brown completely disappeared. Only the whites showed, and like always, the look terrified and fascinated me at the same time.

"Yes sir, I had the boys after me too. But I had to leave it all when my daddy up and moved us to California. I was so scared. Everybody laughed at my clothes and the way I talked, and I hated it here."

I glanced at Trin to see how she reacted to this discouraging news. She looked worried.

"Then I met a couple of real nice girls, just like my Mello and Harmony here," Lottie continued. "They just took me in big as you please, and next thing you know, I had just as many friends as before. So don't you worry your pretty little head none, you hear, Miss—What was your name again?"

"Trin," she answered. Then she stood quietly, suddenly speechless in Lottie's presence.

Harmony ordered and paid for her chocolate mocha freeze quickly, before Lottie had time to start another story. Trin and I followed her example.

We stood at the counter and watched Lottie make our drinks. She talked nonstop. The bell over the door jangled, and in swaggered Makayla, leading her three followers. She tilted her Miss Piggy nose and looked away the second our eyes met.

Lottie said, "I'll be with you in a minute, girls. I've kinda got a rush going."

I whispered to Harmony, "Should we get this to go?"

She quickly glanced back at Makayla and nodded. "We'll take our drinks to go, Lottie," she said, and we leaned against the counter as the Snob Mob shuffled into line behind us.

"Oh, let's stay," Trin said, not even noticing our discomfort. "We just got here, and our drinks would melt outside in a flash. Raise your hand if you hate drinking a frozen drink that's not frozen."

"Sure, Trin, we'll stay," Harmony said. She shrugged at me.

I wanted to remind her about point one of our strategy — avoiding Makayla. Trin was ruining it already, and school hadn't even started.

Then I heard the giggling behind us. It always started as giggling and turned into loud, obnoxious laughs. Most times, we couldn't find the source of their laughter. But today it didn't take a college degree to figure out it had something to do with us.

Harmony and I tried to ignore them by watching Lottie manhandle her blenders, but Trin walked right into their trap.

"Hey there!" she said, whipping around and flashing her mile-wide smile at the enemy. "I'm Trin. I just moved here from ... Hey, why do you guys have your hands up?"

Makayla and her friends answered with complete explosions of laughter.

I shook my head no at Trin. Maybe she wasn't my best friend, but I didn't want to see her trampled by the Snob Mob.

"I get it!" Trin said, her smile getting even bigger. "I said 'raise your hand.' Ohwow, I say that so much I don't even know when I'm saying it anymore. And y'all really did it! That's so cute! So you don't like melted drinks either, huh?" And then she laughed right along with them. For a while.

Actually, once Trin joined their laughter, they didn't seem to think it was so funny anymore.

"So do you guys know each other?" Trin asked, looking back and forth between us and the Snob Mob.

Harmony and I stood there, speechless. Did we know each other? Definitely. But this wasn't the time to explain how mean Makayla had been to us since third grade.

"Of course," Makayla said. "It's Harmonica and Melodious, right?" More blasts of that irritating laugh.

Trin laughed too. "Oh, if you think their names are bad, you'll have fun with mine. Everyone calls me Trin, but my name's really Trinity. So let's see ... you could make it Trinidad. Or Trendy." She laughed again, and they just stared at her. "What are your names?"

Makayla introduced herself, Bailey, Ella, and Jamie.

"So let's see," Trin said. "I think I'll call you McDonald's, Baby, Elephant, and Jammies. So nice to meet you. Thanks for making me feel welcome here."

They didn't laugh.

"That's a way fabulous game," Trin continued. "I'll never get bored again. You girls are so much fun. Ohwow, look, my drink's ready. Guess I better drink it before it melts. We hate that, don't we, McDonald's?" She flashed one more smile at the Snob Mob, grabbed her drink from Lottie, and headed straight for the back booth.

Harmony and I grabbed our drinks and followed her. Somehow I made it into the booth without tripping over anything.

"That was excellent, Trin," I said.

"I can't believe you stood up to the Snob Mob!" Harmony whispered.

Trin just looked at us with big, innocent eyes. "Every place has a group that tries to make other people feel stupid. They won't let you ignore them, so just play their game with a smile when you have to and avoid them when you can."

At that moment something changed inside me. I felt like I might be able to make room in my life for Trin, after all.

Unfortunately, the feeling didn't last.

chapter • 5

• • •

I slurped my frozen caramel cappuccino and listened as
Harmony and Trin talked strategy. Like Trin needed a plan
for cool or cute.

"I have the absolute best idea!" she bubbled. "Ohwow, this
will keep us busy till school starts."

"What?" Harmony asked. "What is it?"

"There's a music-video contest. I saw it on the news last
night. We have to enter."

"Enter?" Harmony asked. "A music-video contest? Don't
you need a music video to enter?"

"That's the point!" Trin said. "We'll make one."

"You mean, we'll be in it? We'll be the band?" Harmony's
gray eyes lit up behind her star-shaped glasses. "Cool
frijoles!"

Harmony smiled at me, expecting me to be excited too.
"How fun is that, Mello? We could be famous!"

Trin turned her look of pity on me. "I'm sorry you don't play violin anymore." Then she giggled. "Not that the violin would fit real well in a rock band. But, honestly, I think Harmony and I sound good enough to try. I thought maybe you could record us."

That sounded excellent. Let me preserve for all time how the new girl is walking in and stealing my best friend.

Trin kept talking. "It would be perfect if we had a drummer. Didn't you say your neighbor plays the drums?"

Now I giggled. "Yeah. I'll talk to him if you want me to."

Harmony's eyes drilled holes into my face, and I knew she was dying to tell Trin I play drums. I shook my head and said, "You can use the shed to practice. When do you want to start?"

"You might want to start now, Trendy," said Makayla. We hadn't even noticed her approaching our table. "Because my friends and I are entering the same contest. We're planning to win it. Since you're new in town, you don't know my dad owns a video-production company." She tilted her nose up and smiled a tight-lipped, totally fake smile.

"Great!" Trin said. "So I guess you're hoping that winning is more about the video than the music, huh? Let's wait and see. Good luck!"

• • •

That night Harmony came for a sleepover after she finished karate and I finished choir. I almost pulled her arm off when she climbed from her mom's gold van.

"Hey, look," I said, dragging her rolling suitcase. "Lamont is shooting hoops. That's convenient."

Harmony yanked my arm to hold me back. "Don't ask him, Mello! Por favor!"

Lamont came dribbling over. "Hey, Harmony," he said. "Welcome home. How was visiting your aunt?"

"Really great," Harmony answered, "and I got spoiled rotten. But no cell signal, so I'm glad she brought me home early."

Lamont bounce passed the ball to Harmony. She had to put her guitar down to catch it. "What is Mello not supposed to ask me?"

I smiled at him and let go of the suitcase. I held my hands out for the ball, and Harmony passed it to me. "Harmony and Trin want to know if you'll play the drums in their new band." I passed the ball to Lamont.

"Cool! I'm really good. Who's Trin?"

"She just moved here from Texas," I answered, "and she thinks Harmony and I need her to plan our lives for us." I didn't mean to actually say that out loud.

Harmony looked disappointed. "Mello! I can't believe you said that. Trin just thought we'd have fun being in a band together."

This time I kept my thoughts to myself. Like the fact that I wasn't in the band. I got to shoot the band.

Harmony picked up her stuff and walked to the door of the shed. "Are we sleeping out here or in your room?" she asked.

"In the shed, but not yet," I answered.

She went inside. I thought she must really be mad, but then she came back with another basketball. "OK. Let's play knockout."

I smiled. "Excellent." Usually I hate sports. I'm just too much of a spaz, and I always lose. But Lamont taught us how to play knockout years ago. The first person in line shoots. If the ball misses, then the next person tries to make a basket before the first person can make it. If the second person makes it, the first person is out. Then the second and third people go. With only three people, a game doesn't last long. Over the years we've added all kinds of rules to stretch it out.

I had to concentrate pretty hard to stay in the game. I let Harmony explain to Lamont about the band.

"So, Mello, why aren't you playing the drums?" Lamont asked.

I missed my shot. "Because I don't play in front of people, Lamont. Duh."

Harmony caught the ball and held it. "Why won't you try, Mello?" she asked.

*Why don't you understand?* I thought. If Harmony does something dumb, she laughs about it. When I do something dumb, I beat myself up about it for months.

I looked around trying to avoid my friend's eyes. "I hate public stuff. You know how I feel about being the mayor's daughter, Harmony. I hate being up front. Why would I do this?"

Harmony sounded irritated. "It's not like it's a live concert, Mello. It's a video. We could shoot it in the shed."

"Yeah," Lamont agreed. "And you're playing drums, not lead guitar. You could practically hide behind that huge drum set."

I shook my head.

"There's something else, isn't there?" Lamont asked.

Suddenly, it didn't feel so good to be with Lamont and Harmony. It felt like they were double-teaming me, or whatever it's called when two basketball players guard one player from the other team.

"Why would anyone want to listen to me?" I said. "There are people who play way better."

Harmony and Lamont looked at each other and shook their heads. "Are you fishing for a compliment," Lamont asked, "or do you really not know how good you are?"

Harmony said, "You are awesome, Mello. It's amazing to listen to you, to watch you."

"Yeah," Lamont said. "How anyone as uncoordinated as you can play like you do — it's really kind of a miracle."

Harmony shoved him, and he faked a big fall. I had to laugh.

"You were born to play the drums, Mello," Harmony said.

I looked at my feet.

"It's Collin, isn't it?" Harmony asked quietly.

I felt the tears filling my eyes. Crud. I didn't want to cry.

I remembered that last summer when I'd sneak into the shed so I could watch Collin play the drums. In my mind, I could still see him there: my big brother. He symbolized "cool" to me.

When I was really little, he'd carry me on his back to the shed and let me push my foot on the bass drum pedal while he ripped across the snares and cymbals just to make me feel like a part of his music. He even played tea party with me — not like other girls' big brothers — until he turned fourteen.

I suddenly became just a clumsy seven-year-old sister. He was too old, too much of a teenager to hang out with me. Mom said he'd grow out of it. I started sneaking into the shed when he played, hiding behind the old sofa just to watch him. I let his music fill me up, hoping someday he might pay attention to me again.

Then that awful Saturday morning came, when I woke up and found Lottie in the kitchen. Mom should have been there making M-shaped pancakes. M for Mello. No C for Collin pancakes that day.

He had spent the night with his best friend, Haydn Smith. Collin thought he was too old for alphabet pancakes, anyway.

I didn't find out what had happened until afternoon.

During the night, the boys decided it would be fun to take the Smiths' car for a ride. They probably weren't afraid, since Haydn drove around the block with his dad sometimes.

They should have been afraid. Haydn made a mistake, and the car flipped over. My brother and his best friend died instantly.

Mom never made C-for-Collin pancakes again. And never again could I sneak into the shed and listen to my brother play. He didn't get a chance to "grow out of it." But I still snuck into the shed. At first, I just sat and looked at the drums. Then, I picked up the drumsticks. I tried to make music for Collin.

It sounded pitiful, but I got better. Then I kind of got obsessed. I played hour after hour, day after day, week after week.

At some point over the years, the music became mine. But it was still my truest connection with my brother.

Lamont's voice pulled me back. "You probably don't want to hear this, Mello, but it's been years since the accident. If you started drumming for Collin, that's cool. But maybe it's time you share it with someone else."

Harmony added, "It doesn't mean you love him any less."

I took a deep breath. "Um, I think I'm out of the game. You guys finish up. I'm going to bed."

Harmony grabbed my arm. "I'm coming too."

I shook my head. "Please don't. I'm too tired to talk. Finish your game, OK?"

I went to the shed and found my sleeping bag. I unrolled it and crawled in. What did Harmony and Lamont know? I didn't think I was that great on drums—or that great at anything. If I tried to be in this band, I'd probably mess it all up. Besides, why should I have to change my whole personality from shy to outgoing just for Trin's stupid idea? And why should I dig up my deepest hurts just because she hauled her guitar in here to take over my life?

I stared at Collin's drums as it got darker and listened to the thud, thud, thud of the basketball. Then I got up and pulled the blue material to the side. Behind it, I found the shelf I wanted. I reached up and felt around until I touched it—a box of old school papers and notes. I got it down and shuffled through until I found my old Bible that I'd saved, the one with Noah's ark on the front.

I may not know what a life verse is, but I'm smart enough to know John 15:16 is a verse in the Bible. I looked it up:

> *You did not choose me, but I chose you and appointed you to go and bear fruit—fruit that will last. Then the Father will give you whatever you ask in my name.*

So that was Trin's life verse. Maybe that meant it was her favorite. I could see why. I thought about Trin—pretty, bold, funny, sure of herself. Everything I have never been. Yeah, I could see why God would choose her.

And what was she asking for? A new best friend named Harmony? A rock band and first place in a music-video contest? With God on her side, who was I to stand in her way?

I crawled back into my sleeping bag, wondering what it would feel like to be chosen.

# chapter • 6

• • •

Saturday

"Buenos dias, Senorita Sleepyhead!"

I opened my eyes to see Harmony five inches from my face. She smiled bigger than anyone needed to before eleven a.m. on a summer day.

I rolled over, away from her. "I hope you have a good reason for waking me up, Senorita Gooberhead."

I felt her pillow hit my back. "I don't know," she answered. "This is the day we go to Water Works. Is that a good enough reason?"

I sat up and started crawling out of my sleeping bag. I noticed Harmony already had on her swimsuit and cover up. "Today? I can't believe I forgot."

Harmony smiled. "We've had a few things on the brain." She looked away, like she felt shy all of a sudden. "Listen, I'm sorry I pushed you about the band. Trin is fun, and I'd love to make that video. But you're my best friend. Forever. That's more important than being in a band."

I gave her a hug. "Thanks, Harmony. I'll hurry up and get ready."

Twenty minutes later we sat in my mom's car, ready to go. Harmony said, "Oh, Mrs. McMann, could we stop by Trin's house, por favor? I told her we could give her a ride."

I tried not to pout, but it didn't seem fair. I wanted us to have this one day to ourselves. If I was her best friend, why did she always want to hang around Trin?

Harmony told my mother where the Adamses lived. Of course, Mom went to the door and talked to Trin's mom for ages.

I got more and more irritated. If we hadn't stopped, we could have gone down the huge yellow waterslide (the straight downhill one that makes me feel like I left my stomach at the top) about ten times already.

Then Harmony had the guts to ask, "What's wrong?"

I didn't answer her. Couldn't she figure it out?

• • •

Water Works is a nifty little park with palm trees and tropical flowers tucked in around the attractions. It has a surfing wave pool, a curving blue white-water slide, a pink "bunny" slide for smaller kids, and — the most popular attraction — a giant yellow straight-down slide in the middle of the park.

Trin and Harmony jawed nonstop while we bought tickets, went through the gates, and got in line for the giant slide.

I stood there, arms crossed, ready to have a miserable day. Then Cole Baker got in line right behind us with his friends Hunter and Karson.

I tried to control myself. I would not stare or do anything stupid. But I did glance back every few seconds to be sure they were really there.

For a year Harmony had tried every possible way to get near Cole. Seeing him on the other side of campus inspired pages of notes in our journals. She had dozens of photos of him she'd snapped with her phone like some kind of secret agent. They were all blurry and distant. Cole on the other side of the cafeteria. Cole at the far end of the hall. Once, Harmony almost had an asthma attack when he and Hunter and Karson came into the Java Joint. And she doesn't even have asthma.

I have to admit, Cole's awesome. I glanced back again and checked out his straight brown hair, big blue eyes, and baby face. This was the closest I'd ever been to the guys. No wonder Harmony spent last year adoring Cole from afar.

I tried to think of something charming to say. Not to the boys, who didn't even know our names. But if I could just say something brilliant to Harmony, maybe she'd notice they were there. Or maybe Cole would notice her. My brain was unable, as usual, to get my mouth to work. But my hands—I couldn't keep them still—kept tapping a rhythm on my legs.

"Are you OK?" Harmony asked. Suddenly, she noticed the boys and whipped her head back toward the front of the line, only to start pulling on her right ear. Harmony, who talks all the time, just stood there grabbing her ear. Not excellent. The first time we've been within fifty feet of Cole Baker and we practically start having convulsions. Definitely not excellent. Not even good.

Trin didn't have a clue. She said, "Ohwow, this place is sweet! And this is a huge slide. But let's go on the blue curvy one next. These ones that go straight down are way scarier. Are you two nervous or what?"

She stopped talking and looked back and forth from Harmony to me. I wanted to say, "I've ridden this slide at least a hundred times. It's my favorite." But my mouth was still stuck shut. And Harmony's ear had turned bright red.

"You poor things!" Trin said. "You both look scared to death. Listen, we don't have to do this slide if you're scared. Let's start with the pink one and work our way up."

Super not excellent. Now we weren't just having nervous fits, we were about to be led off toward the bunny slide like babies.

Trin actually turned to the boys and said, "Excuse me. Could you let us down the steps? I don't think my friends are ready for this slide yet."

Cole, Karson, and Hunter looked at one another like "how embarrassing."

"Sure," Cole said. They scooted to the edge of the stairs.

The situation couldn't get worse. Of course, it was all Trin's fault.

"It's not that bad, really," Karson said.

I looked into his root-beer-brown eyes and said, "Yes it is. It's—oh, you mean the slide."

"Yeah, we've been sliding it all morning." He grinned at me all lopsided and shook his mat with both hands. "Just hang on and keep the water out of your nose."

I managed to speak, "So you think I should try it?"

He grinned again and said, "Sure. You'll be all right."

I smiled back and said, "OK, then. I'll try to be brave." I pulled my eyes away and turned to Harmony. "Let's do it."

Harmony's jaw hung open, but at least she'd let go of her ear.

Still clueless, Trin just said, "Great!" Then she looked at Harmony. "Do you think you can do it? I'll leave with you if you want me to."

Harmony almost choked trying not to laugh. "I guess since Mello is so brave, I can be brave too."

We turned around to face the top of the stairs. If we had gone home right then, it would have been okay, because I knew the day couldn't get any better. But I was wrong.

We heard Cole say, "So practice tonight after dark. We've got to wrap up that bridge if we're gonna tape tomorrow."

Harmony and I looked at each other. No way!

Trin turned around. "Are y'all talking about the video contest for channel 34?"

All three of them puffed up their chests at the same time. "Yeah," Cole answered. "We've been playing since fifth grade. We're KCH—for Karson, Cole, and Hunter."

I felt my hand start tapping again and couldn't believe it when Harmony fluffed her hair and turned back around.

"Which of you is which?" Harmony asked.

They introduced themselves, and we introduced ourselves. Karson actually looked at me and said, "Yeah, I think I've seen you around."

"We're entering the contest too," I said.

"You're in a band?" Hunter asked, shaking a wet black curl off his forehead

"We're just starting one," Harmony answered. "I play bass. Trin plays lead guitar and does vocals."

"And I play drums," I blurted out.

"Huh? I thought—" Trin began.

"Oh, look," Harmony interrupted, "it's our turn!"

The three of us slapped down our mats in separate lanes. The lifeguard raised her flag, and we took off, screaming all the way down.

At the bottom we sloshed through the pool toward the steps. Trin nudged me before we even got out of the water. "What was that about? Why did you lie to those boys? You don't play drums."

Harmony put an arm around my shoulder, and we climbed out together. "Actually," she said, her face beaming, "Mello is the best drummer ever. This is awesome! Our band is going to rock!"

"So why didn't you tell me?" Trin asked. She seemed a little angry. I guess she's not used to feeling left out.

"Mello doesn't want people to know she plays because—"

"Because I'm very shy, and I hate being up front," I interrupted. I elbowed Harmony in the ribs. I didn't want her to say anything about Collin on this perfect day.

"What changed your mind?" Trin asked.

I felt my cheeks get hot. Harmony laughed and asked, "You couldn't guess?"

"Hey!" Karson yelled, wading toward us. "You made it."

"Yeah," I answered. "Great ride."

He bounded up the steps with Cole and Hunter behind him.

"So," Karson said, "you were screaming all the way down. You gonna ride again?"

"Trin wants to try the blue one next," I answered.

"Cool," he said. "Time to surf." He flashed me one more lopsided smile as he and his friends headed toward the wave pool. And Cole looked back over his shoulder toward Harmony and yelled, "See you later!"

"Good luck in the contest," Harmony answered.

They disappeared into the crowd.

I turned to Harmony and squealed. She squealed back, and we held each other's shoulders and jumped up and down.

Then I fluffed my hair and imitated Harmony's voice. "Which one of you is which?"

"Don't even start!" she said, laughing. "What did you say to Karson? 'If a big, strong boy like you wants me to be brave, I will!'"

I threw my arms around her. "Can you believe they stood right behind us?"

"And talked to us?"

"And they're going to be in the contest?"

"So now we'll always have something to talk to them about!"

Trin tilted her head and squinted her eyes at us. You'd think she had never seen us before and couldn't figure out how she ended up with us. "So you like those boys?" she finally asked.

Harmony winked at me. "Oh, I guess they're all right," she answered.

Trin looked my way. "And that's why you decided to join our band? To impress boys? What about your neighbor, Lamont? I thought you were going to ask him to be our drummer."

Harmony laughed so hard she snorted. Thank goodness that hadn't happened in line.

"Listen," I said, "if you guys want Lamont, you've got Lamont. I'll be OK."

"Too late, Mello," Harmony said, wiping her face with the back of her hand. "The word is out, and you are in. I'm telling you, Trin, you'll be amazed. With Mello, we have a chance to win this thing."

"Yeah, OK, great," she agreed, nodding her head. She sounded like she said it to convince herself. "So we need to have a practice, huh? How about tomorrow?"

Did she mean that as a challenge? Well, no problema, as Harmony would say. I couldn't wait until the next day.

I would show Trin what I could do on the drums.

# chapter • 7

•••

# Sunday

We met at the shed Sunday after church. Trin said, "So now we've got a drummer, but we don't have anyone to do the recording or make the video."

Harmony and I looked at each other. At the exact same time we said, "Lamont. Jinx! You owe me a soda. Sorry, the machine is out of order. Please come back and pay me a quarter."

"What was that about?" Trin asked.

"Oh, we've done that rhyme since second grade," I explained to Trin. "Anyway, Lamont is excellent. He's a total geek. His family has a ton of computers, digital cameras, camcorders, and software to do this stuff. He'd love to make our video."

Harmony said, "Cool frijoles. Let's go ask him."

We walked over and knocked at the sliding door on the side of Lamont's house. Lamont's younger sister let us in. Pashay had a book in her hand, as always.

I said, "Hey, Pashay, can we speak to Lamont?"

She looked confused, probably because Harmony and I don't usually go looking for Lamont. Mostly we try to get rid of him.

Pashay finally smiled and yelled, "Lamont, a bunch of pretty girls are here to see you."

She whispered to me, "That's probably the only time I'll ever get to say that to him!"

I heard Lamont pounding down the stairs from his attic bedroom. He came running to the door and said, "Oh. It's just you guys."

"Muchas gracias, Lamont!" Harmony said, putting her hands on her hips. "It's not just us, either. We brought Trin."

"Oh," he said. "Good to meet you. So you're the one who is starting the band?"

She nodded and said, "I'm trying to. I saw it on the local channel, and I thought it sounded so fun! And Harmony is great on bass guitar, and I play lead—"

Harmony interrupted. "Lamont, we're wondering if you'll make our music video."

"You want me to play drums and shoot at the same time? You're finally figuring out how talented I am."

Harmony said, "Mello's going to play the drums."

"Oh, happy day!" he said, giving me a big high five. "I'm proud of you, woman."

I held on to his hand and gave it a squeeze. I know Lamont is a dork, but it felt good to make him proud.

"So, what about the video? Do you think you could make one?" Trin asked.

Lamont tilted his head like he had to think about it. "Why don't you guys come in and see some of my equipment and some of the stuff I've done."

We filed in through the small kitchen and living area into the media room. Lamont's mom sat at one of three computers arranged on a long counter.

"Hello, girls!" she said. "Mello, Harmony. I don't believe I've met you, dear." She held out a hand to Trin.

"I'm Trin. I just moved here from Texas." She shook Mrs. Williams's hand. "Nice to meet you."

Lamont explained about the band and the video.

His mom said, "Well, let me get out of here so you kids have room to work. Call me if you need anything."

Harmony looked around. "Wow, Lamont. Major technology."

Lamont turned on the two computers that weren't already on. Then he turned on a TV on the other side of the room. He sat at the first computer and started typing stuff in. "Here's a Flash piece I made for the science fair last year."

Classical music poured from the tiny speakers, and the computer screen showed a patch of green grass. As we watched, a dandelion shot up above the grass, bloomed yellow, and then turned into a white fluff ball. Next, Pashay's face filled the left side of the screen and she blew. Each little white piece of fluff lifted off the dandelion. The camera focused in on one piece and followed it up into the blue sky. Then the sky turned yellow, orange, and red as the sun set. Finally, just as the music ended, the screen went dark.

We all talked at once.

Harmony said, "Cool frijoles!"

I said, "Excellent!"

But Trin said it best: "You're a genius."

He showed us all kinds of equipment and talked about Linux boxes and terabytes and nonlinear editing until my head started hurting.

Lamont's hands moved as smoothly as a surgeon's with all those computers. Finally, Trin asked him, "So are you in?"

Harmony held up her hand, palm out. "Wait. Before you agree, it's only fair for you to know about the competition. We know for sure some guys from James Moore are entering, but we don't know who's doing their video."

"We'll have to ask them!" I said happily.

Harmony grinned at the possibility.

"The other band we know about is Makayla's," Trin said.

"Have you heard of her dad's company? Simmons Video and Audio Productions?" I asked.

Lamont pursed his lips and drew in a loud, long breath. "Tell me Simmons isn't doing their video," he said.

Harmony tugged on her ear. "Sí, they are. I know they're professionals and all, but are they that good?"

Lamont put his head down on the counter. "Haven't you heard of them? They win national awards. Their stuff is incredible."

Harmony, Trin, and I looked at one another. Maybe Makayla was right. Maybe she did have a better chance to win.

Lamont raised his head. "We can beat them."

"What?" Harmony asked.

"Simmons won't expect anyone else to take this seriously. I bet they won't put much effort into their video. We'll take them by surprise. I've got some awesome new Mac software that I'm dying to play around with."

"So you'll do it?" I asked.

"Yeah. I'm in," he answered.

I gave him a high five. "I'm proud of you, man," I said.

"When is this contest? I'll need at least three months. Six would be better."

Trin started twirling a piece of hair around her finger.

Harmony pulled her ear.

I tapped on the counter.

"Hello? When is this video due?"

Trin finally answered. "Um, the contest is in three weeks."

"Three weeks?" Lamont yelled. "Are you crazy? If I started right now, I couldn't make a decent video by then. Do you have any idea what's involved? Lighting, sound, graphics ... forget it."

"Crud. So what do we do now?" Harmony asked.

Trin kept twirling her hair. "Let me think. Maybe we could get one of those tripod things. We'll set the camera on it. I can turn it on and then run around and get in my spot—"

"Oh, fine," Lamont interrupted. "At least I can hold the camera for you. But don't expect perfection. It will have to be pretty basic."

Harmony grinned. "Great. Meet us at the shed in thirty minutes."

• • •

Trin and Harmony plugged in their instruments. "So now we've got to decide on a song," Trin said. "I like classic rock."

"But won't that be kind of boring?" Harmony asked. "I think we need to do something different to stand out. Maybe an eighties punk sound, or even something with a retro disco beat."

I spoke up. "If we want to stand out, why don't we do alternative?"

Lamont walked in with his camcorder pointed at me. The little red light blinked off and on.

"We aren't playing yet, Lamont," I explained, "and it hasn't been thirty minutes. We haven't even picked a song."

"I can see that. But this background footage will work in nicely. Besides, I need to get familiar with the setting. Just pretend I'm not here."

Trin shrugged and said, "Let's just start with something. How about 'One Day You'll Know'?"

She would pick that song. It has totally boring drums.

Trin gave us three counts, and I started. At first I just kept it basic. Harmony joined in, and we sounded pretty good. Then Trin came in on lead so loud that I couldn't even hear my own drums.

So I played louder. And I made it a little more exciting — you know, more bass drum, more cymbals, and more complicated. It didn't fit the song, but neither did Trin's blaring guitar.

Then Trin started singing. She actually has a great voice, but I think trying to sing louder than her own guitar and my drums messed her up. Her voice cracked on the high notes and faded on the low notes.

After the first verse, Harmony held up her hands. "Wait a minute, niñas. We can do better than this!"

We stopped playing. Harmony said, "Trin, your guitar is way too loud."

"Definitely," I agreed.

Right away, Trin got up in Harmony's face. "But I'm playing lead. Raise your hand if you know what that means. It means I play melody, so it needs to be loudest."

I walked around the drums and stood in front of Trin. "But drums and bass are foundational. Raise your hand if you know what that means. It means without our parts your melody is floating in space."

Harmony turned to me. "Speaking of floating in space, what was that you were doing on the drums? It had nada to do with the song we're playing."

"Oh, please! At least I can improvise. Somebody had to cover up Trin's voice!"

"Ohwow, I cannot believe you just said that! You — you —" Trin stopped talking and tilted her head to one side. "My mom's calling. Just a minute."

She went to her purse and dug out her cell phone.

"Hello … yes … what? Mom, we're practicing. It's our first practice! Yes, I know I promised. I'm sorry. Yes, ma'am … I'll be ready."

She flipped her phone shut and shoved it hard into her purse. "Total bummer. This is so frustrating. Obviously we need to practice, but I have to go. I promised to babysit my little brother tonight."

Harmony said, "Hey, maybe we need a break anyway. No problema."

"We've only got three weeks!" Trin yelled. "We can't afford to take a break. Ohwow, this is such a pain. Mello, you have no idea how lucky you are not to have a brother."

The air rushed out of me like I had been punched. I grabbed my stomach and said, "What an awful thing to say!"

"What?" Trin asked.

Harmony laid a hand on Trin's arm. "Trin, is your mom coming to pick you up?"

Trin nodded.

Harmony said, "I'll walk you out."

I waited until they were gone before I unloaded on Lamont. Poor guy, he just sat in the corner like a mouse in a snake's cage.

"I cannot do this," I began. "I cannot work with Trin. She is driving me insane! Why is she always so sure she is right? And she's so loud and bossy. She wants to run my life and everyone else's."

Lamont just looked at me with his big, black eyes. "Anything else bothering you?"

"Yes," I admitted. "I wouldn't even be in this stupid band if it weren't for Trin. Now we're going to look like idiots. I hate looking like an idiot. I'm going to quit. You be the drummer, and the band will stink even worse than it does now." I regretted my words on some level, even at the moment they slipped out, but I felt too angry to really care. Not in my heart.

"Maybe that's the best thing, Mello," Lamont answered quietly. "If you quit every time something is hard, you'll save your energy. You won't accomplish much, but hey—not everyone can do great things."

"Oh, shut up, Lamont," I answered, hating him and hating myself and maybe everybody at the same time.

"Why don't you just take your camcorder and go home?"

That's what he did. He didn't even look back at me when he shut the door.

I waited ages for Harmony to come back in. She would understand about Trin now. Harmony would give me a hug and say we didn't need Trin or the band. Then everything could be like it used to be.

But she didn't come back. I figured she must have ridden home with Trin's mom.

Finally, I called. Harmony answered and said, "I can't believe you said that tonight. I thought we were best friends. You don't need to worry about me anymore. Ever." Then she hung up.

I thought, *That can't be right. Why is she mad at me? What did Trin do now?*

I called again, and again, but she didn't answer. Finally, I sat down at the drums. But I didn't play.

I just cried.

# chapter • 8

...

The next day I didn't get out of bed. I lay there staring at the watercolor painting on my wall, wishing I could step into it and be in another world. A soft, gentle, pastel world where bad things never happened. A world without a certain pink-haired girl named Trin. I wished for a long time, but it didn't work, so I finally got up.

I got out the quick oats and poured some in a bowl. Then I poured it all back in the container. I wandered out to the shed and started playing my drums. I cranked up "One Day You'll Know" on my iPod and played along on the drums. I beat the drums like a crazy person.

I kept watching the door, hoping to see Harmony. She'd say, "Hello, Mello. I made a mistake. I don't want to be friends with Trin, but of course you're my best friend forever."

After I played two songs, I couldn't stand it anymore. I called Harmony again, pacing back and forth in the shed while I waited for her to answer. But she didn't. I left a message: "If you're mad about what I said about improvising, I'm sorry. You're getting better at it. Come on, call me back."

I waited ten minutes and tried again. I got her voice mail again: "You have reached the voice mail box of—" But instead of saying, "Harmony Gomez," the recording said, "Quit calling, Mello."

I decided to call her house. Her older sister answered. "Hola." Good! Julia likes me.

"Hey, Julia, this is Mello."

"Hola, Mello." She didn't sound happy.

"Is Harmony around?"

"Um, sí. I think so."

She thought? Come on, they share a bedroom!

I said, "Good. She's not answering her phone, and I've got to talk to her. Will you get her, please?"

"Um, un momento."

I waited a lot longer than a minute.

Finally, Julia came back on the line and said, "She doesn't want to talk to you, but she asked me to give you a message. Something like, 'It's not about improvising.' Does that make sense?"

"Yeah. That means it's not my fault she's mad at me. It's all Trin's fault."

"What?"

"That new girl, Trin, got Harmony mad at me. What can I do? Will you talk to Harmony for me, please?"

"I'll try, Mello, but it won't be easy. She said I'm never supposed to say your name again."

This was very bad. Definitely. I IMed her: *RU there?*

No response.

I sent a text message: *Hello? Write me.*

Someone finally knocked. I said, "You don't have to knock, Harmony," as I opened the door.

Trin stood there.

She had a little gift bag in one hand. She had her other hand in her hair, winding a strand around her pointer finger. She reminded me of a balloon a few weeks after the party is over, when most of the air has leaked out and it's small and wrinkled.

She looked like she honestly felt bad about turning my best friend against me.

"Mello, I'm so sorry. Ohwow, I feel like the biggest jerk in the world. I had no idea you had a brother that ... well, Harmony told me what happened. I can't believe I said you were lucky not to have a brother."

Her shoulders drooped a little, and she looked at my feet. "I'll never gripe about my brother again."

"Trin—"

"No. Wait. There's more. I know I haven't been very nice to you, and I'm sorry. It's just that, well, I'm so nervous around you."

"What?" This didn't sound like the sorry-I-stole-your-friend speech I expected.

"You're so beautiful, without even trying. Ohwow, you could wear a plain white shirt and pants and look ready for the fashion-show runway. Not like me. I spend tons of time getting ready and don't look half as elegant as you. And you're so sure of yourself."

I looked around. This had to be another joke. "Are you talking to me?"

"Of course. I mean, I talk and talk and end up saying the dumbest things. You just sit quietly, and then when you do talk, you always say something worth listening to."

I felt so surprised I couldn't think of anything to say back.

She seemed to shrivel even more. "I came over to apologize. And to say I'd love to be your friend. I mean, I really need friends because I just moved here and all. But I know you and Harmony already have each other, so I'm probably just getting in the way. Besides, I can tell you don't like me too much."

She shoved the gift bag into my hand. "Here." Then she turned and started walking away.

"Trin, wait."

She turned back around, and I thought I saw a little spark of hope in her eyes.

I said, "My brother is gone, and nothing can bring him back. But Harmony is the closest thing I have to a sister. Now I'm losing her too. What did you say last night to make her so mad at me?"

"What do you mean?"

"When she rode home with you. You must have said something. I called her last night, and she said she doesn't want to be my friend anymore."

"But she didn't ride home with me," Trin said. "She just walked out to the driveway with me. She told me about your brother, and then she said she had to get back to you, because you'd be really upset."

It didn't make sense. I said, "She never came back in the shed. I stayed in there and waited, even after Lamont left."

If Harmony wasn't mad at me when Trin left, something must have happened while she was on the driveway.

I tapped on my legs and tried to think. What had Harmony told me? "I can't believe you said that tonight. I thought we were friends." Maybe she heard me talking to Lamont. But I didn't say anything about Harmony. I just griped about Trin.

Oh, no!

Harmony must have thought I said all those things about her!

I handed Trin the gift bag. "Keep this for me. I've got to talk to Harmony. Can you wait here?"

"Sure."

"OK. And what you said last night about not having a brother—it wasn't your fault. You didn't know."

"Still—"

"I forgive you."

"Thanks."

• • •

By the time I got to Harmony's, I felt like someone had stabbed me in the side with a knife. I could hardly breathe. Sweat poured down my face, and my shirt stuck to me.

My stomach felt upset too, but not from running. My stomach hurt because I'd lost my best friend, and I couldn't blame it on Trin.

It was all my fault.

Usually, I go in through the garage and let myself in the back door, but I decided I'd better use the front door today. I walked up the short sidewalk.

As I got closer to the door, I prayed a little prayer. I said, "God, I've ruined everything. Please forgive me. And help Harmony forgive me too."

I rang the doorbell.

Harmony answered the door. She saw me and started to close the door in my face. I caught it and said, "Harmony, I think there's been a big mistake."

She opened the door and said, "Sí, there has. I made a grande mistake thinking you were my best friend all these years. Now I know what you really think. I'm bossy. Flashy. Pushy. I try to run everyone's life. I am completely selfish and I want attention. Did I leave anything out?"

Now I felt like a deflated balloon. "Harmony, I didn't say those things about you! I don't think those things about you at all! I was talking about Trin."

"Trin? You think Trin is flashy and bossy?"

"Yes. Well, I did. Now I don't know. Why did you think I was talking about you?"

"Because I acted so mean about your drum playing. And I did push you to be in the band, when I know that's not your thing. And I am flashy—I mean, I love bright colors and crazy clothes. I know how you hate that stuff. You like everything elegant." She started crying. "I thought you had finally had too much of me."

"Oh, Harmony," I said. Tears mixed with the sweat on my face. "I love all that about you. If you didn't push me, I'd never do anything exciting. And I don't want to wear neon colors and checks and stripes, but you wouldn't be Harmony without them. Oh, please say we're still best friends!"

She wiped her nose and pulled me into a hug. "Sí. Best friends. Forever, por favor."

"Definitely."

"So what about Trin?"

"What about her?" I asked, stepping back so I could see Harmony's face.

"I guess you don't like her much."

"Not really."

"Because she's like me?"

"She's not like you."

"Sí, she is. Maybe you could give her a chance. She felt awful about what she said last night, Mello. She didn't mean to hurt you. And think what it's like to be new." She cried some more. "I can't imagine how lost I'd be if I had to move away from you."

"Actually, Trin's waiting for me now at the shed."

"Then go talk to her."

"OK. How about I call you later? Maybe you can come over?"

"Cool frijoles, mi amiga."

• • •

## chapter 9

When I got to the shed, I found Trin sitting on the couch. She jumped up and said, "Mello—"

I held up my hand. "Please, Trin, wait. Um … do you know how to play knockout?"

Her eyes got huge. "You want to beat me up? Harmony must be really mad!"

I smiled. "No, knockout is a basketball game. I thought we could play while we talk. I'm not good at it or anything, but it's kind of fun."

She looked relieved. "Sure. As long as it doesn't involve punching."

After we each made a few shots I said, "Trin, I've been a jerk, and I'm sorry. I thought you wanted to steal Harmony from me."

Trin missed her basket and ran after the ball. She dribbled back. "As if I could! You two are closer than sisters. You're all she talked about from the first minute I met her. She adores you, Mello. Don't you know that?" She shot again and made it.

"I guess, lately, I've been wondering," I admitted. "But we're OK now. So, you want all three of us to be friends?" I held on to the ball while I waited for her answer. I felt sweat dripping down my back. Surely that came from playing basketball in the heat. Why should I be nervous?

"I wish we could," she answered.

I smiled and shot. Nothing but net. "Maybe we could try. I think I'd like to try."

Trin blinked a bunch of times, and big tears started rolling down her cheeks. I put down my basketball and threw open my arms. She put down her ball and threw open her arms. We had a big, sweaty hug.

"Oh, happy day!"

I looked up and saw Lamont filming us. "Lamont! This is kind of a private moment."

He shrugged his shoulders. "There are no private moments for superstars, which is what you girls are about to be. I'm guessing you're back in the band?"

I gave a thumbs-up sign. "I'm in. Will it break your heart to get kicked off the drums a second time?"

He stretched out his arms and turned the camera toward his face. "I hereby record for all time this second rejection of the greatest drummer in the history of the world: Lamont Williams. I refuse any responsibility for the dismal failure the band may face as a result of this action."

He turned the camera back around and said, "I guess I'll be OK."

I kicked at the driveway with the toe of my tennis shoe. "Listen, Lamont, turn that thing off. I want to tell you something."

"No way, woman. I'm recording this apology."

"How do you know I'm going to apologize? What if I wanted to tell you something embarrassing—like, you have a huge piece of beef jerky stuck between your front teeth."

"Oh, man!" he said. He turned off the camera and scratched between his teeth with his fingernail.

I ran over to him and whispered, "I'm so sorry. I treated you like dirt last night."

He looked at his fingernail. "I still didn't get that beef jerky."

"There is no beef jerky."

"In that case, apologize again, for lying!"

"Come on, Lamont. Will you forgive me?"

He looked at the basketball hoop. "That depends. Maybe if you let me win in knockout."

"Let you win is right. You know I could whip you if I wanted to."

He put his camera on the step and picked up a basketball. "But aren't we missing a player?"

"I'm glad someone remembered me," Harmony said, walking up behind us. "Mello, you never called, so I decided to walk over. I thought you and Trin might be beating each other up."

"Harmony!"

Trin said, "She did say she wanted to knock me out. Or something like that."

Lamont picked up a ball and passed it to Harmony. "You can go first. I wish I could tape and show you girls my skills at the same time. But even the mighty Lamont isn't that good."

Trin said, "You're actually going to put your camera down to play ball? I'm impressed."

Lamont dribbled the ball. "You think that's impressive, you should hear me play the drums."

Lamont killed us in knockout. Afterward, while he and Harmony discussed the video, I couldn't resist asking Trin, "So what's in that gift bag you brought?

She laughed and said, "Let's go see." In the shed, she handed it to me. "Open it." Then she grabbed it back. "No, wait, let me explain first. You know how I said my life verse is John 15:16?"

Those jealous feelings came rushing right back when she said that. Did I know the verse? Yeah. It talked about how God chose Trin and would give her whatever she asked for.

Out loud, I just said, "Yeah."

"My best friend from Dallas—her name is Jordan— challenged me to pick a life verse. She said it's cool to have a verse from the Bible that is your special promise. Of course all the promises are for every Christian, so it's not like John 15:16 only applies to me."

I guess I got that part wrong.

Trin reached into her pants pocket and pulled out a little card. She looked at it and read:

> *"You did not choose me, but I chose you and appointed you so that you might go and bear fruit—fruit that will last. Then the Father will give you whatever you ask in my name."*

"That's my verse," she continued. "Jordan knew I was scared to death about moving all the way to California. She thought this verse might help me remember I'm not alone.

As a Christian, I always have Christ. If no one else chooses to be my friend ... so what? Jesus chose me! And he is the ultimate best friend. Also, if I stay in him, then I can count on him to give me whatever I need to bear fruit."

I sat on the couch and asked, "You mean like love and joy and peace—fruit of the spirit?"

"Not just that," she answered. "Being chosen is even bigger. God chose us to know him. It's also about what we do on the planet, how we show others our connection to Jesus. Our fruit is what others can see ... how we show God is growing our lives. Does that make sense?"

"Yeah, sort of ... "

"Listen, all I really wanted to say is ... this gift I brought ..." She dangled it in front of me. "It doesn't have to be your life verse or anything. But it reminds me of you."

She put the bag on my lap. I reached inside and pulled out a Bible verse in a pretty gold frame. It said:

> *And the God of all grace, who called you to his eternal glory in Christ, after you have suffered a little while, will himself restore you and make you strong, firm and steadfast.*
>
> **—1 Peter 5:10**

"That verse made me think of you," Trin explained. "I can't imagine how you've suffered. But Harmony told me your brother was a Christian, and I'm so glad. And she said you are too. God called you, and Christ promises to restore you and make you strong, Mello."

"So being called, isn't that kind of like being chosen?"

"Yeah! Same thing. Sweet, huh?"

I read the verse again. "Yeah," I agreed. "Definitely suh-weet."

Harmony knocked and walked in. "Now that you've chatted it out and we're one big happy familia, I say it's time for some serious celebrating. What can we do?"

"I've got chocolate pretzels in the house," I said.

"Any peanuts?" Trin asked. "I love peanuts."

"No, Trin, we never eat peanuts," I reminded her.

Harmony licked her lips. "Chocolate pretzels. Serious treat. Or we could hit the Java Joint."

"No, no, no," Trin said, her smile lighting up the shed. "This is bigger than chocolate pretzels or peanuts. It's even bigger than the Java Joint. This calls for a trip to ... the mall!"

I groaned.

Harmony jumped up and down. "Sí! Es muy bueno. Major shopping. We can choose something to wear onstage!"

I panicked. "What stage?"

She looked around the shed. "OK, so maybe there's no stage. But you know—something to wear when we do the song for the video."

Lamont stepped through the open door. "Sounds great. I'll bring an extra battery for the camera."

"Did that male person just invite himself on our shopping trip?" Harmony asked.

Lamont turned the camera on and started filming.

Trin said, "Lamont, we asked you to make a music video, not a documentary. You're not filming the story of our lives."

He focused on her. "Look, the tape is due in three weeks. You don't even know what song you're playing. I've got to take whatever I can get, OK?"

I thought of a compromise. "Why don't you come for the first twenty minutes, and then promise to leave?"

"Do you think I want to be seen hanging out with you? I'm going to get in, get some shots, and get out."

Trin looked at Harmony and me. "But we've been playing basketball. We can't be seen at the mall like this." She pointed at me. "I'm sure Mello could look totally glam in ten minutes, but I'm going to need at least forty-five."

"Let's meet back here in an hour, OK?" Harmony suggested.

Lamont put down the camera. He ran his hand over his head. "I hope an hour is long enough. I'll just die if I don't have time to do my hair! I agree with Trin. I simply can't be seen at the mall looking like this."

Trin picked up a pillow off the couch and hurled it at him. It hit him right in the face.

"I'm leaving, I'm leaving," he said, picking up his camera and darting out the door.

Trin stood up. She said, "Hello? The mall is calling." She helped me up off the couch. Then she put an arm around each of us and pulled us into a huddle.

"We've got to think of a name for our band," Trin said. "In the meantime, everybody yell 'shop till you drop.'"

I rolled my eyes. But then, in the spirit of new friendship, I smiled and put my right hand in the huddle on top of Trin's and Harmony's. They whispered, "One, two, three," and we all yelled, "Shop till you drop!"

I had a feeling this wasn't going to be a typical boring trip to the mall.

• • •

## chapter 10

Still Monday

"Just say it, Mello. You think this shirt is tacky."

Harmony stood in front of me. I could see our reflections in the full-length mirror. "I've just never seen purple, hot pink, and yellow combined like that," I finally managed. "And those sleeves—they look like someone shredded them from the elbows down."

Trin burst out of the dressing room and ran to the mirror. "Harmony! Ohwow, that shirt is fabulous! I love the colors. And those sleeves will look great while you're playing guitar." She did an air-guitar solo right there in front of the whole store. She waved her head from side to side, pink hair flying.

Harmony smiled. "Look at yours, Trin! It really sparkles under the lights." She joined in, dancing around and even making guitar sounds.

Two ladies walking by stopped to watch them.

I headed back to the dressing room.

"Wait, Mello," Trin called. "Let us see what you picked out."

I turned around slowly.

Harmony said, "Come over here."

I sighed and walked back to the mirror.

Trin looked at my shirt. "It's a white T-shirt." She made white T-shirt sound like something nasty.

"Yes, but feel it," I explained. "This material is wonderful. It's so soft. And look — it's kind of shiny."

Trin looked down at her own shirt. Blocks of gold sequins and silver glitter covered most of the black material. Bright pink beads wove in and around the whole thing in crazy patterns.

She pinched a gold section and held it out toward me. "This is shine, Mello." She pointed to my shirt. "Raise your hand if you can say boring."

Harmony spoke up. "You don't understand, Trin. For Mello, the shimmer makes that T-shirt pretty bold."

"Thank you, Harmony," I said, glad she understood.

But she didn't. She begged, "Mello, por favor, choose something exciting just this once. You need to look like a rock star."

"I'll find you something," Trin offered.

"I'll help," Harmony said.

I moved away from the mirror and leaned against the wall. From my post, I could see rack after rack of hideous clothing. Half of it we had already ruled out because it wasn't modest. I didn't have much faith that they'd find something in what was left.

I could also see Lamont. Of course he had the camera running.

I flipped my phone open and checked the time. How long would they make me do this?

In a few minutes they came back, arms full of shirts on clanging hangers.

Harmony tried to hand me a lavender silk one with feather trim.

I refused to touch it.

Trin held up a red satin shirt with black lightning bolts.

"No way," I said.

Sunshine yellow with huge red roses.

"Nope."

Brick red with metallic gold stripes.

"Nuh-uh."

Black and white racing flag pattern.

I grabbed my stomach. "Please, Harmony, you know I can't wear this stuff."

"But you have to try to work with us," Harmony said. "We're a band. We have to work together."

I looked at the two of them. "Let's talk about working together," I said. I took the rest of the shirts out of their arms and dumped them on the floor. Then I stood them side by side in front of the mirror. "Do your shirts look good together?"

"Ohwow, she's right," Trin said. "We totally clash. I guess you better find something else, Harmony."

"What? I picked mine first. It's major cool. Why don't you find something else?"

"I'll never find a shirt as awesome as this one," Trin said, crossing her arms. "Besides, I should set the tone for the band. I'm on lead guitar, and I'm the one singing."

Harmony held both hands up in front of her. "Oh, mi amiga, stop right there. You want to do this music video alone? Bueno. You have fun with your guitar and your shiny shirt, diva."

I heard Makayla's voice before I saw her. "Look," she said. "I knew we didn't have to worry about their band. They can't even choose shirts without getting in a fight!"

The Snob Mob came around a clothes rack and into view. Makayla looked past us into the mirror and fixed her hair.

Ella actually smiled at Trin and said, "Cool shirt. We haven't figured out what we're wearing, either."

Makayla rounded on her. I half expected her to punch Ella, but she just said, "It won't be a problem for us, though, will it?"

Ella looked down. "No. We'll find something great."

"Of course," Makayla said, sticking that nose of hers in the air. She looked down her nose at the piles of shirts on the floor. "But not here. I don't think this store has anything good enough for our band."

Bailey looked confused. "But Makayla, this is your favorite store."

Makayla tossed her head and stomped off. "It used to be."

Her followers did what they do best — they followed.

Lamont stepped forward and said, "I've shot enough for today. This has been real, and it's been fun, but it hasn't been real fun. I'll check you girls later."

"Let's take a break," Trin said. "We'll find shirts eventually." She smiled, stuck her nose in the air, and did a perfect imitation of Makayla's voice: "And it won't be a problem for us, will it?"

"Glasses!" Harmony yelled. She darted away from Trin and me, headed straight for the specialty shop.

Trin looked at me and said, "What's that about?"

"Harmony loves glasses the way most women love shoes," I explained. "She doesn't even need them. Her eyesight is perfect. I guess that's a good thing, because she can get cheap glasses right off the rack."

Harmony already had on a new pair. They had rectangle lenses. "Cool frijoles! I'm buying these."

"How about these?" Trin asked. I turned to look at her and started giggling.

She had on a hideous pair of glasses with thick black plastic rims.

"I'm getting these," she said. "They're only five bucks."

"Just don't ever wear them in public," Harmony begged. "They give glasses a bad reputation."

Trin ignored her. "And look at this!" she said. She held up a tall, skinny bottle. "Spray-on highlights—in blue! Mello, you absolutely must have blue hair for our video!"

"Oh, no," I said, shaking my head. "Never."

"Well, I'm buying it," Trin insisted.

"That's your issue," I said with a shrug.

They bought their glasses and hair color. As we walked out, Harmony sniffed the air. "I smell . . . " We rounded a corner. "Cookies Galore!"

Trin looked at the picture of a huge cookie on the sign above the counter. "Ohwow, a peanut butter cookie sounds so good right now!"

"Peanut butter?" Harmony asked. "Why would anyone get peanut butter when you could get triple chocolate chunk? I'm ready for major chocolate."

I stepped up to the counter. "I'd like a medium milk, please."

Trin said, "You're ordering milk at Cookies Galore? Raise your hand if you think that's just wrong. Get a cookie, Mello, or I'll have to hate you."

I smiled at the guy behind the counter. "A milk and a gingersnap cookie sandwich." I turned to Trin. "They have the best frosting. If you order a sandwich, they put the frosting between two cookies."

"Much better!" Trin said with a nod. "I guess you're OK, Mello."

Harmony flopped down on a bench in the middle of the mall. Trin and I sat on either side of her with our cookies and drinks.

It felt good to relax.

After a while Trin said, "Hey, Harmony, I'll trade you bites."

"OK."

They traded bites, and Trin turned away from us.

Harmony looked at me and shrugged.

Trin turned around. She had on her new ugly glasses, and we started giggling again. Then she smiled a goofy smile. She had a chunk of Harmony's black cookie over one of her front teeth so it looked like it had been knocked out.

In less than two minutes Trin had transformed herself from completely beautiful to completely goofy.

I laughed so hard I fell off the bench.

Harmony laughed so hard she had to cover her nose, because she had soda coming out of it.

Karson, Cole, and Hunter chose that exact moment to come around the corner.

I stopped laughing and hopped back onto the bench. "The boys!" I whispered. "What are they doing here?"

Harmony grabbed a napkin and went after her nose with desperation. "The mall is a public place, Mello."

Trin—crazy Trin—she kept her glasses on. She kept the cookie on her tooth. She smiled and waved at those boys!

They laughed and kept on walking.

"Take those off!" I told her.

She turned back to us. In a hillbilly voice she said, "What fer? I feel downright purty in my new glasses." She looked at me. "OK. I'll take them off, but only if you promise to spray on blue highlights for the video, Mello."

Harmony and I started laughing again.

"You are evil!" I said.

She crossed her arms.

"OK, I'll do it. Now take them off!"

She did.

I dug a pen out of my bag and made a circle on my napkin. I wrote a #1 sign in the middle and put the word goober under it. I tore out the circle, left two long strips of napkin connected to it, and tied the pieces together so they made a huge loop.

"It's official," I said, getting up and standing in front of Trin. I hung the fake medal around her neck and said, "You are the biggest goober of all time!"

Harmony took a picture, then clapped and said, "Congratulations!"

Trin used that hillbilly voice again and said, "This is the downright happiest moment of my life. I ain't never won no awards before now."

"At least something good came out of this shopping trip," Harmony said.

"Yep," Trin said, nodding. "I found out I am number one at something."

"Besides that," Harmony insisted.

"What?" I asked.

"Trin and I both have new glasses we can wear for the music video."

*And I have blue hair,* I thought with a despairing sigh.

• • •

## chapter 11

"Number twenty-five," Lottie yelled.

Harmony went to the counter to get her sandwich.

"Why is she calling out numbers?" Trin asked. "We're the only people in the whole restaurant. She could say our names."

I nodded. "Yeah, and she's known me since I was six. I don't know. It's a Lottie thing."

Harmony came back with her Tuscan chicken wrap and chips. "Are you talking about the numbers?"

"Yeah."

"I think it's her way of making you feel special for ordering real food. She doesn't do numbers when you just order a drink."

"Number twenty-six."

Trin laughed and walked to the counter for her turkey and sprouts.

I picked up my tray and breathed deeply. Lottie makes a serious veggie delite sandwich.

"I'm glad to see you eating your veggies, honey," Lottie said. "Those veggies make you strong." She stopped and looked at me. "You already look stronger somehow, Mello."

I smiled as I walked back and moved my plate and glass from the tray to the table. I don't like eating off those trays. I sat down across from Trin and Harmony, picked up my sandwich, and opened my mouth for a big bite.

Something didn't feel right. I looked up. Harmony and Trin sat there, staring at me.

"What?" I asked.

"I asked Harmony if we could pray before we eat," Trin said.

I put my sandwich down and looked around. No one else had come in, so it was still just us. "Oh, definitely," I said. "We always pray before meals at home."

Trin held a hand out to Harmony and me. I looked at Harmony. She shrugged, took Trin's hand, and reached for mine.

I held their hands, bowed my head, and closed my eyes.

I heard the bell jangle above the door. Someone came into the restaurant. I forced myself to keep my eyes closed.

"Dear God," Trin prayed, "thank you for Harmony and Mello. I couldn't have chosen better friends. And thanks, most of all, for choosing us. Amen."

I looked up.

Lamont stood there, pointing his camera at us. "This is more like it," he said.

Harmony shook her head and said, "Lamont, you have no respect."

"You are totally wrong about that. I have all the respect in the world for people who respect God and each other. You'd rather me stick to shooting your fights at the mall?"

"Let's not bring up yesterday," I said and then took a huge bite of veggie delite.

"Still no outfits for the video?"

"No," Trin admitted. "But Harmony and I got new glasses."

Harmony started shaking with laughter. She had a mouth full of soda, and I could tell it was going to either spray out of her mouth or shoot out of her nose again.

I tried to help her. "Swallow, Harmony. You can do it." But I started laughing too, so that made it worse.

Harmony turned red and fanned her face with her hands. Finally she managed to swallow.

Trin and I clapped and cheered.

"You people scare me," Lamont said. He went to the counter.

"We really do have to decide what to wear," Trin announced, munching on her chips.

Harmony took a bite, wiped her hands with her napkin, and got a notepad out of her purse. "If you could wear anything at all, what would you choose, Trin?"

"Well, I love layers," she answered. "And different textures of material. Um, I like short, filmy sleeves. And I adore anything that laces up — boots, shirts, whatever."

Harmony scribbled on her notepad. Then she held it out to Trin. "What about something like this?"

"Ohwow, how did you do that?" Trin screeched. "You've drawn my dream outfit! It's killer!"

Harmony sparkled with happiness. "I love designing clothes. What about you, Mello? If white and cream tees are outlawed, what else could you see yourself in?"

I chewed a bite of sandwich and swallowed. "Maybe a very, very pale blue tee," I said with a grin.

"Number twenty-eight," Lottie yelled.

Lamont grabbed his food, sat in the booth next to us, and started cramming his sandwich down his throat.

Harmony's pencil flew around the page. I had a feeling she wasn't drawing a T-shirt.

She held it out for me to see. She had drawn a crossover shirt made from two different types of material. It tied on the side in a loose bow. The bottom of the shirt hung down over cropped-legged pants.

"I actually likc it, Harmony," I admitted. "It's excellent."

She clapped her hands. "Now for me." She let us watch while she drew a T-shirt with contrasting sleeves and ruffled edges. Next she drew a fringed miniskirt over flared knee-length pants.

Trin covered her mouth. Then she hugged Harmony. "Ohwow, you are a total genius! It must be so fun to be able to do that. Put them side by side."

Harmony tore the pages out of her notebook and lined them up.

"They look great together," she said. "Too bad we can't wear notebook paper."

Lamont stood up and looked at the pictures. "Too bad the outfits won't make you sound any better."

"Ohwow, that's rude!" Trin said.

"Just trying to keep you focused. I thought you wanted a band, not a fashion parade."

Harmony gave him a look. "First things first. When we know we look good, we'll be free to focus on our music. You obviously don't understand the female mind."

"You can say that again!" Lamont said.

All three of us said, "You obviously don't understand the female mind."

Then Harmony and I added, "Jinx. You owe me a soda. Sorry, the machine is out of order. Please come back and pay me a quarter."

Lamont shook his head. "Wow. Yeah, you women are way too mature for me. Just remember I didn't mean any disrespect by filming your prayer time. I'm not sure you realize what kind of power you're tapping into when you pray." He looked at his camera and then back at us. "Oh, happy day! I just got a seriously awesome idea for the music video."

He headed for the door.

"What is it? Tell us!" Trin said.

Lamont started walking back. His face glowed with excitement. Halfway to our table he stopped. "No. I'll wait until your clothes are ready and you know you look good. Then you'll be free to focus." He turned back toward the door.

Harmony wadded up a napkin and threw it at him. "Goober!"

Lottie yelled, "Hey! None of that! Don't make messes in my restaurant! You clean that up right this second!"

"Yes, ma'am," Harmony answered, getting up to get the napkin. Lamont made a face at her before he ran out.

I looked at the papers still spread out on the table. Then I looked at Harmony and Trin. "I could make these," I said.

"Mello! Cool frijoles! Of course you can!"

Trin looked at us and said, "Huh?"

"Mello sews," Harmony explained. "She's really good too."

Trin looked at Harmony. "So you design clothes." She looked at me. "And you sew clothes." She held out her hands and looked at them. "Raise your hand if you think Trin missed out on the skills. All I do is buy clothes and wear clothes."

"Oh, no, mi amiga," Harmony corrected. "Surely you haven't forgotten you play lead guitar and sing."

Trin blushed. "Yeah, whatever. So could you make these clothes right away, Mello?" she asked.

"I know!" I said. "Let's go to the thrift store. We could buy some basic things that I can turn into this stuff."

Trin looked doubtful. "The thrift store? Aren't those clothes … used?"

Harmony and I laughed. "Oh, Trin, you've got a lot to learn."

• • •

We stood in line at the thrift-store checkout. "I still can't believe this place!" Trin said. "I'm getting three shirts, a skirt, pants, a belt, and boots for less than twenty-five dollars! That's less than one pair of pants at the mall. Ohwow, we have to shop here from now on!"

I put my pile on the counter, and the worker started ringing it up.

"It's fun, isn't it?" Harmony asked. "Especially when everything with a green sticker is half price. I knew you'd catch on, mi amiga."

Trin looked at the clothes in her arms. "Mello, you really think you can turn these clothes into what Harmony drew?"

"Yeah, I think I can. At least I'll get close. It's going to be fun."

"So here's the big question," Harmony said. "I'm almost afraid to ask."

I gathered up my bags, and the worker started in on Harmony's clothes.

"What?" Trin asked.

"Well, we haven't had a fight all day," Harmony pointed out. "Are we brave enough to try another practice?"

I froze. Trin froze. Harmony glanced back and forth from me to Trin.

Our last practice almost ended our band and our friendship. I looked at my feet. Trin shuffled her sandals.

"We've got to do it sometime," Harmony said.

Fortunately the cashier interrupted by handing Harmony her bags and change.

"What do you think, Mello?" Trin asked. I lifted my head.

"OK. Tonight," I answered.

"Thanks again," the cashier said. "You girls have a nice practice!"

We pushed through the exit doors. A nice practice. I had my doubts.

• • •

## chapter 12

# Still Tuesady

I sat at the drums and messed around, working on my speed and hand control. I wanted this practice to go well.

I think Harmony and Trin felt the same way. They didn't even talk. They just plugged in and started tuning.

Harmony spoke up first. "Where'd you find these lyrics, Mello?"

I looked at the yellow paper in her hand. "Oh!" I said, jumping up. I ran and grabbed it from her.

"I've never heard that song. Or is it a poem?" she asked.

I stuffed the paper under a stack of magazines. "I . . . um . . . it's nothing."

"It sounds muy bueno. How does the tune go?"

I went back to my drums. "I'm not sure. I don't remember."

Trin finished a riff and looked up from her guitar. "Let me see the lyrics. Maybe I could make up a new melody for them."

I tapped on the toms, throwing in a boom on the bass drum after every third beat. "Nah. Let's do something else. How about—Harmony, what are you doing?"

She dug around under the magazines and came up with the paper. "Here it is. Read it, Trin."

Trin let her guitar hang from the strap around her neck. She took the paper and read:

*"Oh hear my song*
*And make me strong*
*Sometimes I feel like I could fall.*

*Show me your face*
*I need your grace*
*To be the person you have called.*

*Get so confused*
*But I know You*
*Will be there through it all.*

*I can see everything my life can be.*
*YOU'VE CHOSEN ME*
*And in my soul*
*The words you speak*
*They set me free*
*To hope, to dream, to really breathe*
*To live the truth that I believe*
*And now I know the meaning of your love"*

Trin looked at me. "Hey! That sounds like the verse in First Peter."

I couldn't help smiling. "I thought so too. First Peter five, verse ten." I winked at her. "It's my life verse."

Trin smiled too, and it looked like the smile came from deep inside her – like she smiled with her whole self. "Sweet."

Harmony looked at Trin and me. "I think I missed something."

I said, "It's something Trin and I talked about instead of beating each other up the other day."

Trin laughed. "Yeah. I can't believe you found a song that's based on your life verse, Mello. I want to hear it. Do you remember who sings it?"

I felt my face getting hot. I looked away and started a steady tap on the snare. "Um, I'm not sure."

Trin walked over and waved the paper in front of my face. "You made this up, didn't you?" she asked. "Ohwow, Mello! I didn't know you wrote lyrics." She looked at Harmony. "Is there anything Mello can't do?"

I snorted in surprise. I'm not exactly used to people thinking I'm talented.

"She can't play basketball worth a flop," Harmony offered, smiling.

I stuck my tongue out at her before I said, "It's worth a flip, not a flop."

She laughed. "Fine. You can't play worth a flip-flop."

"What is a flip worth, anyway?" Trin asked.

"I don't know, but this practice isn't going to be worth a flip either if we don't get started," I said.

Harmony took a deep breath. "I'm kind of afraid to start. Our last practice didn't go so well."

"That's an understatement," I agreed.

"Can we pray before we try again?" Trin asked.

I looked at Trin's face. She was serious.

"I'm used to praying before meals and all, but ... " I shrugged my shoulders.

Trin said, "If it's OK to ask God to bless our food, why not ask him to bless our practice?"

Harmony walked to the middle of the room. "Makes sense to me," she said holding her hands out to us.

Trin took her guitar off and laid it on the couch. She stood by Harmony and took one of her hands.

They both looked at me.

I said, "I don't like to pray out loud, you know, in front of people."

"You don't have to," Harmony said, reaching for me. "We'll pray."

I walked over to them and took their hands. I closed my eyes and bowed my head. No one said anything for a while, and I felt every beat of my heart.

I thought, *This feels pretty strong, coming to God like this.*

Finally Trin prayed, "God, here we are: Harmony, Mello, and me. We're just three regular kids, but you are the almighty God. And you have chosen us! Thank you for calling us."

"We want to please you with our music and with our lives," Harmony prayed. "Please help us. Amen."

Both girls squeezed my hands, and I knew they were finished.

I squeezed their hands but kept my eyes closed. I cleared my throat. "Thank you for these excellent friends. Thank you for making us strong. Amen."

Trin and Harmony echoed, "Amen."

I looked up. Trin and Harmony both had red, watery eyes. I guess I did too.

Trin laughed and pulled her hands away to wipe her nose. I ran over and grabbed the tissue box.

Harmony pulled out a tissue and blew her nose, loud. It sounded like a goose honking. That got us all laughing, and then we really started crying.

"Why are we bawling our heads off?" I asked.

Harmony took off her glasses and wiped them with another tissue. "I think we're blown away. It's amazing to think that God knows the three of us are here, you know? And that he would choose us."

"Definitely," I said. "The chosen girls."

Harmony and Trin snapped their heads around and stared at me.

Trin yelled, "Ohwow, raise your hand if you think that's the name for our band!"

Harmony pulled us into a hug. "Sí! It's perfect."

I hugged them back. Then I stepped away and held my right hand out in front of me, palm down.

Harmony put her right hand on top of mine.

Trin put hers on top of Harmony's.

We didn't even have to say what we were going to do. We pumped our hands up and down three times and yelled, "the Chosen Girls rock!"

"Oh, happy day!"

We looked at the door. Lamont stood there, recording us. He said, "Don't panic. I just got here. I think I missed something good, though."

We smiled at one another. "Yeah, you did," Trin agreed.

"I know. You must have decided what to wear."

Harmony shook her head. "Oh, please. Don't be so shallow, Lamont."

"Still no costumes, huh?" he asked. "Please make that a priority. I don't see how you'll be able to focus today. I mean, you don't even have your clothes ready. You don't 'know you look good.'"

Harmony did a roundhouse kick (and the yell that goes with it) in Lamont's direction. "You might want to take that back, Lamont. We always look good."

Lamont looked at Harmony, posed to strike again. "Um, I'm thinking I'll catch you later," he said as he left.

Trin said, "Let's try something totally different today. How does this sound?"

She hummed a few bars and then added the words I had written. The melody sounded beautiful, but more like a ballad than a rock song.

"Could we speed it up?" Harmony asked.

"What if we start off slow and soft on the verse, but then do this on the chorus?" Trin said. She sang the chorus faster, in a bold voice, and rocked out with her guitar.

"Cool frijoles!" Harmony said. She picked up her bass and started figuring out her notes.

I sat at my drums and found the beat. The snares and cymbals worked well for the verses, and I added the toms and bass during the chorus.

I also echoed Trin on vocals. She looked surprised at first, but then she nodded and smiled. I broke into an alto line, like we'd always sung together.

Of course we had to stop and start over a few times until we got it all figured out. But it sounded excellent, and we knew it. The air felt electric.

"This has to be the song we do for the video," Trin declared. "Can we practice again tomorrow? I promised I'd babysit my brother tonight."

Harmony said, "Yeah. Maybe Mello and I can work on the costumes for a while."

"Definitely," I agreed.

Trin laughed. "Lamont will be pleased."

• • •

Harmony draped a piece of bright orange cloth over her head. "This looks muy bonita with my purple shirt, don't you think?"

I threw a wad of black material at her. "I have an idea," I said. "We could wear sweatbands and leg warmers for the video. That way we'd be the queens of fitness and the queens of rock and roll at the same time!"

She fell onto my bed, laughing. "Those leg warmers looked so bad on you."

"Whatever! You better be careful what you say while I'm working on your skirt." I ran the sewing machine back over a few stitches and cut the threads. Then I held up the finished product.

Harmony grabbed it and danced around the room. "Super cute, Mello. You are one cool girl."

"You designed it," I reminded her.

Harmony stopped dancing. "We're muy bueno together, aren't we?" she asked.

"Like chocolate and pretzels," I agreed.

Harmony cut, and I sewed until finally the costumes looked just like her sketches.

"Let's put ours on!" Harmony said.

We stood in front of my full-length mirror. Harmony pranced like a model on a runway, and I even strutted a little.

Then Harmony started playing air guitar, and I played air drums.

"Hey, I like that song you wrote," Harmony said, swinging her arm in a huge arc.

I kept drumming in the air. "Thanks."

"I'm glad we started a band," she said, kneeling down for a dramatic finish.

I hit an invisible cymbal. "Me too."

What? I stopped drumming and looked at myself in the mirror, surprised. Because it was true—I really did feel glad about the band.

I hoped the feeling would last.

# chapter • 13

•••

Three days and eight practice sessions later, we waited for
Lamont to arrive with the camera.

"Why isn't he here?" Harmony asked. She flopped onto the
couch and popped the lid off her bottle of orange juice.

Trin sat on the carpet, sipping bottled water. "Yeah. He
hasn't recorded a thing since Tuesday. I thought he needed
every second he could get."

I poured my water into a glass of crushed ice and took a
drink. "Remember the last time, Harmony? You went ninja on
him."

Harmony sat up. "Did he think I meant it?"

I shook my head. "No. I called him this morning. He said
he'd be here. Send him a text message." I stood up and tried
to make the bow on the side of my shirt smaller, but that just
made the ribbons hang down longer. I wished I could tuck
them into my pants. And the pants—how had I let Harmony
talk me into adding lace to the cuffs?

I refused to even think about my blue hair.

"Mello, you look really nice."

I looked up and saw Lamont smiling at me. He didn't have that smart-aleck look on his face like he does when he teases me. He looked like—like he was proud of me. Something in his eyes reminded me of Collin. Would Collin be proud of me and the Chosen Girls?

I managed to say, "Thanks, Lamont" and get behind my drums before I had to wipe my eyes.

Trin said, "OK, Chosen Girls, let's rock."

"Wait!" Lamont said, "I've been thinking about the set. We can do some simple stuff that will have a big impact." He dragged the coffee table and positioned it in front of Trin. "Mello, do you have any more of that blue cloth?"

"Definitely. In that red plastic box on the shelves."

He draped some fabric over the coffee table. "Can you stand on this and feel safe, Harmony?" he asked.

She grabbed her bass and stepped onto the table. "Wow! I'm the tallest for once," she said happily. "This will work."

Lamont went to the shelves again and came back with some wooden crates. "Is it OK to use these, Mello?" he asked.

"Sure," I answered.

He laid four of them flat and pushed them together. "Try standing on these, Trin."

She stepped up carefully, like she thought they might break. "I don't know. Sometimes I jump around and stuff."

"Try it," I encouraged. "Those boxes are really strong."

She did a tiny practice jump, and then a bigger one. "OK. I'm good."

"Usually we'd put the drums higher in back with you guitars down in front, but we don't have anything big enough for your drum set, Mello. Actually, this looks pretty cool," Lamont said, nodding.

Trin said, "So, Chosen Girls, now are we ready to rock?"

"No!" I said. It came out louder than I meant for it to.

"What now?" Trin and Harmony asked.

I walked out from behind my drums and stood in the middle of the room. I held my hands out to them.

Trin smiled, stepped off her boxes, and grabbed my right hand. Harmony hopped down from her table and joined us.

I said, "I'll pray." We bowed our heads. "God, you've given us your promises, and you've given us a song to sing about them. Help us do it well. Amen."

Then we put our hands in the middle. "One, two, three. Chosen Girls rock!"

We took our places, and I tapped four beats.

We went straight through the song. We kept smiling at one another, because we were acing it. Not a missed note, not a single wrong word.

When we got to the chorus, Trin looked up as she sang, "You have chosen me." It was beautiful — like she sang right to God.

It made me think, even while my arms and feet kept busy with the drums.

I thought, *I used to play the drums for my brother. Then, for a long time, I played for myself. When I played for Trin, it was just to show off.*

I looked up too, and between verses I whispered, "This is for you, God."

After the last note faded, Trin jumped off her boxes and screamed, "Ohwow, that rocked!"

"Cool frijoles!"

"Excellent!"

"Oh, happy day!"

Harmony looked into the camera Lamont still had pointed at us. "So you can turn that off now, right? We're finished, sí?"

Lamont laughed and clicked off the camera. "Actually, we need to shoot it about six more times, so I can get different angles. Afterwards, I'll get some shots of each of you alone. And I need you guys to all wear the same color for that. "

"What for?" I asked.

"Humor me. I'm an artist."

I groaned.

We did the song, or parts of it, seven more times before Lamont was satisfied. Then he sent us off to change clothes.

We each came back dressed in all white. It was the only color the three of us had both a shirt and pants in.

"Trin, you first," Lamont said. "Stand up on your boxes with your guitar."

She did.

"Now hold it like this," he said, pulling her guitar out in front of her and making the strings face the wall. He stepped back and shot for a while. Then he left and came back with a trash can lid and a broomstick. "Hold this lid in front of you with your left hand, and hold the broomstick up high like this with your right."

I laughed. "You look like the cleaning lady warrior! She defeats all dirtiness."

"You can come clean my room anytime, warrior," Harmony added.

"Why am I doing this, Lamont?" Trin asked.

"No questions. Harmony, you'll be next."

He made Harmony do karate moves. Then he said, "You hold the broom in front of you with both hands—aim it right at me."

"I'll aim it at you, all right," Harmony joked.

When it was my turn, Lamont just stared at me and my drums. Finally he said, "Aha! Stand up and hold your sticks together above your head. Good, good. Now bring them down and jab them at the air."

"Lamont, have I ever told you you're weird?" I asked, jabbing away.

Lamont looked like he really thought about it. "Only four hundred and thirty-two, no, thirty-three times," he answered.

I laughed. "Let's make it four hundred thirty-four."

"Wait a minute," Harmony said. "You told us we had to wait until our clothes were ready and then you'd tell us about the video. They're ready, so you should tell us what all this weird stuff is about. Now."

Lamont said, "I did say that, didn't I? Sorry. I changed my mind."

• • •

## chapter 14

"Where you girls been?" Lottie yelled so loud her voice almost drowned out the blender.

"We've been working on our music video," Harmony explained.

"Oooh! I wanna see it!" Lottie said.

Trin said, "Yeah. So do we."

Lottie handed Trin a strawberry banana smoothie. "What do you mean? Why can't you watch it?"

"Lamont is holding it hostage," I explained, taking a slurp of frozen caramel cappuccino. "He's doing something weird, I think. He won't show us."

"We've begged for days," Harmony added, resting her elbows on the counter. "You know what I want."

"Chocolate mocha freeze," Lottie said with a smile, loading the blender again.

"Waiting is the worst part," Harmony said.

"I'll ask him." I got out my phone and typed: *What's taking so long?* Then I reminded Trin, "He said he'd keep it basic."

"I hope it's not too basic, though," Trin said. "I don't know. Maybe it wasn't fair to ask him to go up against Makayla's dad. He's a professional."

I thought, *It's a little late to worry about that now.*

Harmony grabbed her drink, and we headed for the back table. Just as we slid into our seats, the bell on the door jangled.

Lamont walked in. "There you are!" he said, heading our way. "I've been looking for you guys. I thought you might want to see the video."

We all screamed. I almost spilled my cappuccino, and Trin asked, "Can we watch it right now?"

Lamont shook his head. "No. Sorry." He slid into the booth next to me.

"You dork," Harmony said. "You walked all the way down here to tease us about the video, and it's not even ready?"

"Did I say it isn't ready?" he asked.

Trin crossed her arms and narrowed her eyes. "So it's ready, but we can't watch it?"

"Did I say you can't watch it?"

"Yes," I said, frustrated.

"Trin asked if you could watch it right now," Lamont explained. "You can't watch it right now because there isn't a computer in the Java Joint. But if you'll walk up to my house—then you can watch it."

We screamed again, sucked down our drinks, and headed for the door.

The California sunshine washed over me as I scrambled to keep up with Lamont on the jog home. I wanted to yell at him for being such a goob, but I couldn't catch up with him. Only Trin matched his pace the whole way.

At his house, he led us into the media room and sat us down in front of the biggest computer monitor.

Harmony pulled on her ear, which by now should have hung down like the ears of those people in *National Geographic*.

Trin looked like she was making dreadlocks. She hissed at me, "Shhh! You're making me nervous."

"I didn't say anything."

She pressed my hands still against my legs.

Okay. So maybe I felt a little nervous too.

Lamont turned around. "Can I get you anything? Coke or popcorn, maybe?"

Harmony just growled, "Lamont."

He said, "OK, OK. Just trying to be a good host. So I guess you want to see it, huh?" He rubbed his hands together and took a few deep breaths.

*He's afraid!* I realized.

"Lamont, it will be great. We'll love it," I assured him. "Remember, our other option was a tripod."

"Right," he said. "Listen, I need you to do one thing for me. Watch it one time through without asking any questions or making any comments, OK?"

"Definitely."

"No problema."

"Fabulous—of course."

He stalled a little more. "I know I said I'd keep it basic, but I got this idea. I kind of got carried away, maybe, but it seemed—"

"Could you just let us see it?" Trin asked.

He nodded. "Here goes."

He flipped off the light in the room and pointed the remote at the TV.

One shiny soap bubble floated across the black screen. When it got to the middle, it burst. The words The Chosen Girls: "You've Chosen Me" emerged from the bubble and got larger until they filled the screen.

"Cool frijoles," Harmony whispered.

"No comments," Lamont reminded us.

"Sorry," Harmony said.

Then three still shots of each of us showed up, side by side like school pictures. Under my picture it said:

**Melody "Mello" McMann**
**Drums**
**Backup vocals**

Each of the three portraits had a label like that.

Then the front shots changed to profiles. It made me think of mug shots on crime shows. I almost giggled. Had Lamont forgotten to make this a music video?

Our photos disappeared, and I let out a tiny scream. Where our faces had been, three monsters, or maybe demons, looked out at me.

The first one had skin the color and texture of a hedge apple—bright green and knobby all over. Its eyes were green too—algae green.

Under the picture it said:

**Jealous E.**
**Discourage trust**
**Focus on what others possess**

The second monster-thing looked slimy, gray, and wrinkled. Under his picture it said:

**Rival Ree**
**Promote competition**
**Discourage cooperation**

The last creature had beautiful, jewel-like skin, but super-creepy eyes shooting red laser beams. Its label said:

**P. Ride**
**Encourage self-importance**
**Promote vanity and conceit**

The screen went fuzzy and gray. I heard the beats that signaled the beginning of the song. As the fog began to clear, I could see myself tapping on the rim of the snare and then playing. Next, I saw Harmony at the left of the screen totally into her bass. Finally, the view widened to include Trin on the right. She gently plucked notes on her electric.

Her voice sounded soft and pure on the first words:

*"Oh, hear my song … "*

I heard my echo,

*"Hear my song … "*

We sounded like angels. Then at the side of the screen appeared the prickly green monster. Jealous E. rolled like a ball to my drum set as the music continued. It stood up and the tiny spikes grew longer from its skin, until it shot a spike that struck me on the arm and fell away.

I rubbed my arm, expecting it to hurt.

The scene changed to a close-up of me in Trin's face, yelling at her during that awful practice. I remembered telling her someone needed to cover up her singing.

I glanced at Trin — she stared straight ahead — and turned my eyes back to the screen that had already cut back to our singing:

*"And make me strong . . . "*

Then the red-eyed shiny creature — P. Ride — scrambled across the bottom of the screen, stopping in the middle and growing taller till it towered over Trin, even on top of her boxes. The thing put his nose in the air and shot red lasers down from its eyes. Red circles glowed on Trin's forehead.

The music continued, but the scene cut quickly to Trin at the shed, in Harmony's face. She was yelling and frowning, with Harmony looking like she could cry.

*"Sometimes I feel like I could fall . . . "*

Back to the band. The last monster — Rival Ree — slithered from behind Harmony and put its short arms up on the table, flicked out a snakelike tongue, and bit her ankle.

Instantly, the screen cut to Harmony at the mall, hands up in frustration, shrieking at Trin. But we heard only the music.

The scene shifted again, panning the Java Joint then zooming in on the three of us at a table, holding hands and praying.

*"Show me your face . . .*

Then us in the shed, holding hands and praying again.

*"I need your grace"*

On the screen, Trin stood with her face lifted up, her mouth open wide in song. At last, the music matched the graphics. Harmony's eyes were shut, her fingers nimbly roving across her bass. And me on the drums. Somehow Lamont had caught my whispering to God.

*"To be the person you have called."*

There in Lamont's family room, Harmony took my hand and squeezed it.

I thought, *This is more like it, Lamont. No more nasty monsters, please.*

Then I gasped, because our video seemed to turn into a horror show. On the screen, we kept playing and singing.

*"You've chosen me ... "*

The three monsters appeared simultaneously, and each separately moved toward its target.

*"And in my soul*
*The words you speak*
*They set me free ... "*

On the screen, glitter sparkled around us, swirling like in a snow globe. Trin spun around twice and was suddenly clothed all in white, brandishing a sword and shield. She blocked P. Ride's lasers. She aimed her sword at the shiny monster, and bolts of lightning blasted until it fell back, withered, and disappeared.

At the same time, Harmony did a crescent kick and lifted her bass like a kite in the wind. When she jerked it down, it turned into a sword, and she too wore a white suit. She held her sword in both hands and leveled it at Rival Ree. The creature cowered as a lightning bolt shot toward it, and it disappeared from the screen.

Jealous E. faced me. My white suit had a huge cross on the front. My drumsticks turned into a sword, and I held it high above my head and then swung it toward the prickly green thing. Again, the light from the sword made the monster disappear.

Suddenly, on the screen, we looked like ourselves as we continued the chorus:

*"To hope, to dream, to really breathe*
*To live the truth that I believe*
*And now I know the meaning of your love*
*You've chosen me."*

The screen went black as the music ended.

"Ohwow, that's just too intense!" Trin finally said.

Harmony said, "I'm impressed, Lamont!"

"It's excellent," I told him with a smile. "Definitely."

He flopped into a chair, looked up at the ceiling, and let out a long breath. "I am so very good," he said. Then he looked at us. "But I guess it's time to see what the judges think."

chapter • 15

• • •

Saturday,
Two weeks Later

Trin, Harmony, and I sat in the auditorium chairs and watched the Snob Mob file into the seats right in front of us. The moment they got settled, Makayla turned around and said in a sugary-sweet voice, "I hope you don't take it too hard when we blow you away."

Trin smiled. "We'll try to be strong," she answered.

I looked around the huge room. Hundreds of people had shown up at the recreation center for the music-video award ceremony. I text messaged Harmony: *i didn't know this was such a big deal.*

*sí,* she sent back. *is it 2 late 2 tell them we want 2 drop out?*

Lamont paced up and down the aisles.

"Oh, crud," Trin said, snapping her fingers.

"What?" Harmony asked.

Trin smiled. "Those boys are here, and I forgot my way fabulous glasses."

"Where?" Harmony and I asked at the same time.

Trin kept her hand low and discreetly pointed her thumb behind us and to the left.

We casually glanced over our shoulders.

Yep, they were there.

"Cole's wearing his red shirt!" Harmony said happily.

The lights dimmed and then came back on.

"What happened?" I asked.

Trin bounced up and down in her seat. "It's a warning to find your seat. It's about to start."

Lamont ambled up the aisle. He stopped and shook hands with an older man in a coat and tie. They talked for a minute, and then Lamont dropped into the seat next to mine.

"Who's that?" I asked.

"Mr. Simmons of Simmons Video and Audio Productions," he answered in a soft voice.

"Makayla's dad?"

"Unfortunately for us, yes. I told him I admire his work. He said his company enjoyed working on the video for his daughter's band." He dropped his face into his hands. "I'd hoped he'd assign the project to an intern who'd never held a camera. No luck."

The lights dimmed, but this time they stayed off.

The spotlight focused on a man in a suit who walked to the podium and said, "Welcome to the first ever channel 34 HPTN Music Video Awards."

Everyone clapped.

"We know you're excited that our station is taking this step. Channel 34 is committed to adding more entertainment programming to our lineup, and tonight's contest is just the beginning!"

He made about a hundred announcements and introduced all the big shots, including my dad.

"We're pleased to have Hopetown's mayor, Mr. Wes McMann, here this evening," the man said.

Dad joined him in the spotlight and shook his hand.

"Mr. McMann, is it true that your daughter entered a video in tonight's contest?"

I scrunched deeper into my seat.

Trin flashed me a thumbs-up. I looked away.

Dad smiled and stepped to the mike. "Yes, she did. We're very proud of Melody. And if the judges know what's good for them—" Dad stopped talking, and everyone laughed, as if on cue. I couldn't have been more embarrassed if I'd left my pants at home.

"Seriously," Dad continued, "the judges have promised not to show my daughter's band any preferential treatment. Best of luck to all competing tonight."

Dad left the stage as the crowd erupted in applause. The announcer said, "And now—the awards!"

A screen bigger than a garage door lowered behind him.

"We hope to make this contest bigger and better every year," the man explained. "But for this, our kickoff year, we have two categories. The adult category is for anyone eighteen or over. The youth category is for anyone under eighteen. We'll begin with the youth category."

Harmony grabbed my hand and squeezed it, hard.

"In third place, we have KCH!"

We screamed and clapped as we turned to watch the guys. They jumped up, pumped their fists, and half jogged to the stage.

The KCH video started, and the boys' faces filled that whole huge screen. I thought Harmony might pass out. For sure, I lost circulation in my hand because she just about squeezed it off.

"Breathe," I reminded her.

I thought, *I will so die when they put my face up there.*

The boys rocked, and so did their video. I felt proud to kind of know them.

The announcer introduced them and gave them a two-foot-tall gold trophy. He asked if they wanted to say anything. Karson and Hunter shook their heads, but Cole stepped up to the mike and said, "Thanks."

Everyone clapped as the boys went back to their seats.

"In second place ... Real Romantics." High-pitched screams erupted on the other side of the auditorium. Two girls who looked about twenty ran to the stage.

Makayla turned to Bailey and yelled above the applause, "That means we won!"

Harmony's mouth fell open. "Oh! They are so cockney!"

"Be quiet," I said. "Cockney means from a certain part of England. You mean cocky," I corrected.

The Real Romantics video — all lace and roses — ended, and the band took their trophy and left the stage.

The announcer said, "And first place in the youth category goes to —"

My stomach felt like right before I head down the yellow slide at Water Works.

"Makayla Simmons!"

In front of us, the Snob Mob shot up like rockets and screamed and jumped around and hugged and cried. Before they headed to the stage, Makayla took the time to flash her paper-thin fake smile at us and say, "Sorry."

Harmony let go of our hands. As soon as the Snob Mob looked away, she covered her face.

Trin just shrugged, smiled, and said, "We tried."

I patted Lamont's arm, but he didn't notice. He just stared at the screen.

I wanted to hate Makayla's video. But I couldn't. It had great special effects, and their singing actually sounded decent.

I hadn't even wanted to form a band, but now I felt my heart breaking.

Harmony uncovered her face and started watching. "Why is the name of their band Makayla Simmons, when it has four members?" she asked.

"Do you really have to ask?" I replied.

After the video, Makayla accepted the three-foot-tall trophy and made a speech. She went on and on thanking Simmons Video and Audio Productions and even had her dad stand. It sounded like a commercial.

Harmony whispered, "Maybe they should have called the band the Simmons Video and Audio Productions Band. I don't mind losing, but I wish we didn't have to lose to them!"

"I bet we had more fun than they did," Trin said.

I nodded.

We went silent as the Snob Mob pranced back to their seats. Makayla turned around. "Do you want to hold the trophy?" she asked Trin.

Trin smiled. "That's sweet of you, but no thanks. I'm afraid I might drop it."

Makayla held it up. "Yeah, it is really, really heavy!"

The Snob Mob bragged on themselves all through the adult category awards.

After the adult winners got their trophies, the announcer did the typical closing stuff. I tugged on Harmony and pointed to the exit. We had already put up with the Snob Mob long enough — I didn't want to chat with them afterward.

She and Trin started gathering their purses and programs.

I bent over to get my purse, only half listening as the man onstage said, "And one final award. Best Overall Video goes to … the Chosen Girls."

I jumped in surprise and whapped my head hard on Bailey's seat. I heard my friends' surprised exclamations.

"Cool frijoles!"

"Ohwow! Sweet!"

"Oh, happy day!"

But even as we ran to the stage, dragging Lamont with us, it was too unreal to believe. Before we got to the steps, our video began. It filled the huge screen, and I didn't feel embarrassed at all.

Our music blasted through the whole auditorium. The building pulsed with energy, and the crowd clapped to the beat.

I couldn't keep still. I threw an arm around Harmony, and she grabbed Trin, and then I even put my other arm around Lamont. The four of us swayed back and forth, singing our hearts out with the video.

I looked at the crowd rocking out to our song. Then I looked behind me at the screen, where we turned into superheroes and fought off the evil monsters.

I thought, *It will never get better than this.*

Somebody shoved a trophy at us and asked who would like to speak. I took a huge step back. Harmony shook her head. Trin stepped to the mike and said, "Ohwow! This is so sweet! We want to thank Lamont Williams for turning us into superheroes. We thank our families, our friends. And thank you, HPTN. But above all—me, Harmony, Mello—we thank God, who called us and chose us."

• • •

In the crowded foyer, my mother put her arm around me and squeezed my shoulders, almost too hard. Then my dad pulled me into a big bear hug and whispered, "I'm proud of you."

I heard Makayla talking to a young man in a suit. "I told you I wanted to win this thing, John! I expected your best work, but you let some dorky guy beat us. That does not look good for Simmons Video and Audio Productions. I'm assuming my dad will cut your next bonus."

Harmony walked up. I nodded toward Makayla and asked, "Should we offer to let her hold our trophy?"

Harmony laughed. "No, she might drop it. It's very heavy!"

I heard someone say, "Congratulations, Mello!"

Karson stood there grinning his lopsided grin.

I looked into those root-beer-brown eyes and said, "Yeah, you too. Great job. Your video was awesome."

"Thanks, so was yours," he said. "Where's that Lamont guy? I want to ask him about his graphics."

I pointed to Lamont, and Karson headed for him.

Harmony elbowed me in the ribs. "So, mi amiga, are you glad you decided to join our band?"

I smiled. "Oh, yeah," I said. "Definitely."

•••

"Is the antenna hooked up yet?" Trin asked.

"Is there any reception?" Harmony asked.

Lamont peeked over the back of the TV. "What do I have to do to earn your trust? It will be ready in time, and there will be reception, unless I get interrupted by any more superheroes."

I carried a dish to the coffee table and said, "For tonight's celebration, we eat out of a crystal serving bowl instead of out of the bag."

Harmony reached into the dish. "Hey!" she said. "Somebody mixed peanuts in with the chocolate pretzels."

Trin sat up. "Peanuts? I just love peanuts!" She looked at me. "But Mello, you said you guys never eat them."

I smiled at her. "We never used to," I answered. "But sometimes change can be a good thing."

"Don't some people call peanuts goobers?" Harmony asked. "That sure fits. Goobers are the goober's number one snack."

Lamont's voice came from behind the TV. "I'm surprised there's still room for a TV in here, with that trophy filling up the place." The TV came on, and Lamont found channel 34. "What do you think now, women?"

"I never doubted you, Lamont," I said as I plopped down on a pillow in front of the couch and grabbed a handful of our new all-time favorite snack.

He finished just in time. The female anchor said something about the weather, and then the male anchor said, "And tonight we'll introduce you to the grand-prize winners of our first music-video contest: the Chosen Girls." Our picture flashed onto the screen.

"That's us!" Trin screamed.

Harmony yelled, "Cool frijoles!"

I said, "Be quiet! We can't hear what they're saying."

" —a music video that is literally out of this world," the man said. A short clip of the video ran. It showed all three of us battling monsters while the chorus played.

"Wow! These girls are obviously not your average teenagers," the lady said. "Channel 34's own Sandy Diaz caught up with them at the first ever channel 34 Music Video Awards night."

There we were on TV, receiving that huge trophy.

Next, we stood beside Sandy Diaz who had her arm around Lamont. "This is Lamont Williams, the young mastermind who put the video together. How did you think of the superhero idea?"

Lamont smiled at her and said, "I watched them try to work together." The camera zoomed in on his face as he said, "And it didn't go well at first, but when they tapped into a supernatural power, and they managed to overcome their problems, the idea just came to me."

"Great! You sure did a good job," Sandy said. "Trin Adams, I understand you are new to Hopetown and you'll be going to school at James Moore."

Trin nodded and smiled an extra-big mega-smile.

"How do you feel about starting at your new school as a rock star and a superhero?"

"Ohwow, I'm so excited! I just know it's going to be a great year," she answered.

"We're glad you moved here, Trin," Sandy said. "And Harmony Gomez? How long have the Chosen Girls been a band?"

Harmony giggled. "A few weeks," she answered.

"That's amazing," Sandy said. "You sound like you've been together for years. You girls are really talented. And there is one more member of the Chosen Girls—Mello McMann."

"Mello, your friends tell me you didn't want to be in the band at first. But you did a great job, and your band won best overall. How do you feel now?"

The camera zoomed way in, so my face filled the whole TV. With a smile almost as big as Trin's I said, "Excellent. It feels great to be chosen."

CHECK OUT this excerpt from book two in the Chosen Girls series.

# DOUBLE-BOOKED

zonderkidz

Created by Beth Michael
Written by Cheryl Crouch

# chapter • 1

...

The scariest moment of my life? My first time in the James Moore cafeteria.

I searched frantically for an amiga.

I practically heard the clock on the wall ticking. I could only stand there holding my tray for so long.

I didn't dare sit next to the windows. I'm not an outcast, but I'm not one of the Snob Mob, either.

I finally spotted some girl I remembered from third grade. I walked over, said "Hi, I'm Harmony," and sat down. She didn't even smile, but it beat sitting alone.

Anyway, all that happened ages ago.

This year my best friend Mello is in my lunch. So is our new friend, Trin, who moved here this summer.

*We're not sitting by the windows or anything, but becoming rock stars and superheroes over the summer didn't hurt us any.*

*So, I'm thinking this is going to be the best year of my life — if Trin and Mello don't drive each other loco . . .*

• • •

I played a repeating pattern on my bass guitar while we waited in the shed for the TV film crew.

"Cool frijoles!" I said. "I'm so pumped. I set the DVR to record channel 9 already, just in case they come early."

"Channel 9?" Mello asked, dropping her drumsticks. "I thought Doc Wazzup was on channel 6. My parents are recording channel 6!"

"Run! Tell them to change it," Trin yelled.

"Fine," Mello snapped. "Just don't be so bossy in front of the TV guys."

Even though Mello's house is only fifty feet away from the shed where we practice, it made me nervous to see her heading out the door.

*"Uno momento,"* I cried. "Use my cell. He could be here any minute."

Mello made the call, tossed my phone back, and flounced onto her big tan couch, separated from Trin by a pile of throw pillows.

"I am definitely not excited about this," Mello said. "I wish we could just get it over with." Then, for the third time, she asked, "What time is it?"

"It's two minutes since the last time you asked," Trin answered, whapping Mello's shoulder with a pillow. "Raise your hand if you think Mello is the only person in the world who doesn't want to be on TV. Ohwow, I can't believe Doc Wazzup is coming to the shed! Is my hair OK?"

"Definitely," Mello answered. "It's still pink and perfect, just like the last time you asked—two minutes ago!"

I actually felt glad to see Lamont appear in the doorway. Mello and I used to send her next-door neighbor away, but those days were as ancient history as elementary school.

"What about mine?" Lamont asked, rubbing his black curly hair, so short you could almost see his scalp. "I didn't have time to do much with my hair today."

Trin threw the pillow at him with a hard overhand, but Lamont ducked, and the ocean-blue missile sailed above his head.

It smacked Doc Wazzup right in the face. I almost dropped my guitar.

Our famous guest took a step back and put his hands up like a shield in front of him. "Hold your fire," he said. "Is it safe to come in?"

"Ohwow, I'm so sorry," Trin answered. "I didn't mean to hit you in the face. I mean, I didn't mean to hit you at all. I meant to hit ... Ohwow." She hid her face in her hands.

I elbowed Lamont out of the way and held out one hand to the TV host. He didn't look much taller than me. I looked into his bright blue eyes and said, "Welcome to the shed. I'm Harmony—a big fan of yours."

He smiled and shook my hand.

Doc didn't look like a TV news anchor. He didn't have a million-dollar smile. (His teeth were a little crooked.) He didn't have slick black hair. (His was light brown and a little messy.) He looked more like somebody's big brother.

I thought, *That's why everyone loves him.*

Chosen Girls is a dynamic new series that communicates a message of empowerment and hope to Christian youth who want to live out their faith. These courageous and compelling girls stand for their beliefs and encourage others to do the same. When their cross-cultural outreach band takes off, Trinity, Melody, and Harmony explode onto the scene with style, hot music, and genuine, age-relatable content.

# Double-Booked

Book Two • Softcover • ISBN 0-310-71268-8

In *Double-Booked*, Harmony finds that a three-way friendship is challenging, with Trinity befriending a snobby clique and Melody all negative. Through a series of mistakes, Harmony unwittingly unites the two against her and learns that innocent comments hurt more than you think. Ultimately, the Chosen Girls are united again in time to sing for a crowd that really needs to hear what they have to say.

**Available now at your local bookstore!**

## Unplugged

Book Three • Softcover • ISBN 0-310-71269-6

The band lands a fantastic opportunity to travel to Russia, but the "international tour," as they dub it, brings out Trinity's take-charge personality. Almost too confidently, she tries to control fund-raising efforts and the tour to avoid another mess by Harmony. But cultural challenges, band member clashes, and some messes of her own convince Trinity she's not really in charge after all. God is. And his plan includes changed lives, deepened faith, and improved relationships with her mom and friends.

## Solo Act

Book Four • Softcover • ISBN 0-310-71270-X

Melody needs some downtime—and the summer youth retreat will really hit the spot! But a last-minute crisis at camp means an opportunity for the band to lead worship every morning, plus headline the camp's big beach concert and go to camp for free. Too busy and unhappy, Melody makes some selfish choices that result in the girls getting lost, sunburned, in trouble, and embarrassed. Can she pull out of the downward spiral before she ruins camp—and the band—completely?

**Available now at your local bookstore!**

## Big Break

Book Five • Softcover • ISBN 0-310-71271-8

The Chosen Girls are back! As opportunities for the band continue to grow, Harmony can't resist what she sees as a big break ... and what could be better than getting signed by an agent?

## Sold Out

Book Six • Softcover • ISBN 0-310-71272-6

Dedicated to proving herself to others, Trinity gets involved in organizing the school talent show. Before she knows it, she accepts a dare from Chosen Girls' rival band, with the winner to be decided by the outcome of a commercial audition.

## Overload

Book Seven • Softcover • ISBN 0-310-71273-4

Melody discovers a latent talent for leadership that she never knew she had. When she begins a grief recovery group for kids like her, she loses her focus on the work God is doing through the Chosen Girls.

## Reality Tour

Book Eight • Softcover • ISBN 0-310-71274-2

When the Chosen Girls go on their first multi-city tour in a borrowed RV, Harmony's messiness almost spoils their final show. What's worse, she almost blows her opportunity to witness to her cousin Lucinda.

Available now at your local bookstore!

## Chosen Girls Music CD

Join Trinity, Harmony, and Melody as they catapult from garage band to superstars, bursting on to the scene with style and hit pop music. Hear song samples on ChosenGirls.com

Available from Provident.

## Chosen Girls Stationary Gifts

• Stickers   • Jotter Notebook   •Note Pouch

Available from Dayspring.

**Available now at your local bookstore!**

We want to hear from you. Please send your comments
about this book to us in care of zreview@zondervan.com. Thank you.

ZONDERVAN.com/
AUTHORTRACKER
*follow your favorite authors*